The Fate of Adolko

The Lanterncup series

Marcus Tay

Author: Marcus Tay (13 years old)

Printed in the

United States of America

@2016 Tay's Imagination World.

ISBN #: 978-0-9964830-6-3

To all, I mean everybody

Contents:

Prologue: Need of Action

"Is he dead?" "The Breaker? I'm afraid so." The Colonel stood on his balcony and stared out at his domain. His mind was wandering off as he thought hard.

He pointed at the horizon as the sun started to sink, and muttered several phrases which were spoken so softly that none a foot and away could understand.

"Um, Colonel? May I suggest an idea that may please you?" said the Adviser. "Yes, what is it you want to speak to me about? It better be good, or it might cost you your life," the Colonel asked, eager to hear.

"I think we should just abstain from any activity for now as we strengthen our forces," the Adviser smiled.

"Ahem, say that one more time slowly and clearly, and pronounce every syllable as if each is its own separate word," the Colonel ordered abruptly. The Adviser was taken aback at these words and knew his master was irritated. "I am sorry if I have offended you...but here it is again," the Adviser said. Halfway through the sentence, the Colonel stopped him.

"Do you really believe I will take a single idea from your mind and use it for the most difficult thing ever going to be done in all history? When we were under the rule of His Majesty, no goal he promised to meet was met. Zero. I was the one who actually kept him alive. He enjoyed life selfishly. He never did a thing that helped and supported us."

"But one day, just that one day, I made the wisest decision in my life to overthrow him so I can take us to farther heights."

"Do you agree?"

"Yes, sir," the Adviser replied. "Did you think I was lecturing you?" "No sir," the Adviser hesitated, not meeting the Colonel's eyes. The Colonel relaxed.

He leaned forward on the balcony fence and rested his forehead on his hand. He stroked his temples as if his pondering was not going to end. The Colonel grunted as he stood up again. The Adviser stood by his side behind him. "What should I do?" "Look, I know my ideas are different from yours, and it is okay," the Colonel pointed out. "What I believe is that we need to actively send out our forces and start conquering land and make them to be our own."

"It will not be easy, I assure you. Nothing will be an impediment of my empire!" the Colonel cried into the air.

"Everything that was once supposed to be mine should still be! All the rules should have been set by me! Every continent should have been governed by me till this day. Do you see why I am so mad?" the Colonel turned to his Adviser. The Adviser reacted anxiously and couldn't say anything.

"Oh, why do I have people like you in my domain? Why do people like you always get the better stuff even if you didn't work hard for it? You, my Adviser, should not rule with me after I take the world. I will find somebody better, more intelligent, and aggressive than you!" The Colonel turned his hand so the underside was showing. He waved it through the air from left to right. "I will not need assistance anymore!"

"You know why we need to hurry in taking over the world? When that Lanterncup fellow gets back to his home city, he will tell everyone about us. But the truth is, we are already too late. My first target will be Yart. It shall fall quickly and I will have my forces hunt him and his friends down. He will be devastated. After that, it will be pretty much over."

"How is one boy your main obstacle?" the Adviser questioned. The Colonel's tone changed suddenly. "No! Not at all! You don't need to know…" "Also, one more thing, why do you keep saying 'My'? Shouldn't it be 'Our'?" the Adviser asked. "Oh yes of course…and I will not need any more help from you!"

"But then, what about me? What should become of me?" "You are, for now, or maybe another eternity, fired permanently!" "What? How could you?"

The Adviser drew out his sword.

The Colonel thrusted his hand and clasped them around his neck.

The Adviser gagged. The Colonel brought him onto the fence and took out a long can from his belt with a rounded top.

"Ah…leave the side of your master and turn against him even after you have made an oath to him? This is not faithful allegiance or loyalty. This is also going against you own word and being untruthful to yourself for the sake of your job! You deserve punishment!" There was nothing on the can. But there was a button on the top. "You should be ashamed!"

The Colonel pressed it and out came green gas that went all over the Adviser's face. It was like spray paint.

The Colonel let go and the Adviser plunged to the depths below.

"Krakum, my signature weapon," the Colonel announced, twirling it in his hand. "Fresh out of my laboratory! Soon it shall bring me fame, power, and accolades! I hope the masses will admire me for my invention! For if they do not, they really have no taste."

"I shall cause fear for man, they will not like it and respond. But when they do…they have endured on a one way trip to their deaths. They will pay for their tickets to death. Watch out humanity, I am coming. Let Zark be the spark of a new northern hemisphere war!" The Colonel spoke all this to himself.

Chapter One: The Grocery Store

Home was the place most comforting above all according to Ian Lanterncup. But it was also the place he lost his father. Ian was well over the tragedy.

An entire month had passed since the loss of Joe, a comrade he had for the whole trip. Ian's school got the news and were saddened. But they quickly hired a new janitor.

Ian knew he had a deeper responsibility ahead of him, but for now, what about some time to just sit on your coach, look out the window of you ranch-style house, watch the birds sing and fly, and sip some sweet tea?

That was exactly what Ian did.

But just experiencing nature was not enough to get his mind off the fact that The Haunter was real, and the entire trip was worthless. Shadow Clan had not accepted their gift, the Crystal of Len. They wanted another favor to be met, but Ian and his friends have had enough. Just remembering the moment, made him very disturbed and it troubled his brain.

The temperature outside was in its 60s and 70s, the best for humans.

"Mom! I am going outside to fly my kite! It is windy!" Ian cried in a monotone voice. He drank the last bit of sweet tea and hurried to the only garage.

The kite was red but had green stripes. It looked as if it had not been used for a long time because there were many wrinkles and it had much dirt and dust.

Ian pulled it off a rack and loosened the string from the handle. He pressed the button that lifted the garage door and ran moderately into his backyard.

His house was located in a rather rural area outside of the suburbs. It was better to live here because there was more land to roam about and not much city-life like cars honking feet from your front door.

Ian found himself close to a tree and as the wind howled, the kite gradually went upwards towards the sky.

It was a day with nice weather and tiny puffs of cloud here and there. They were like little dots of white in a vast blueness.

Ian enjoyed being at home, where he could do almost anything he wanted. Ian could relax the whole day!

But his outdoor activity was soon dismissed with a sun-shower. I have a solution, Ian thought. He snatched his raincoat off a hook and slid it on. Ian put his kite back and again, got himself outside.

While he trudged around his front yard, a noise startled him. He turned and saw his mom, Lorry, knocking on the window and making a 'come back in' gesture with her hand. Ian groaned as always.

When he walked through the front door, Lorry yelled, "Wait! Take off your shoes first! They are mud-stained!"

After that, Lorry demanded, "Ian, go take a shower and cleanse yourself." "Why did you tell me to get inside?" Ian argued. "I will tell you later, but now go rinse yourself at least!" Ian frowned and started up the stairs.

"One more thing," Lorry shouted from beneath, "Don't take too long, the water bill is always expensive!"

Ian had not showered for weeks. He felt sticky from dried sweat.

Ian got a new pair of clothes, went into the bathroom, locked the door, got ready his towel, and turned on the water.

While inside, he had not felt so warm and cozy for a long time. Ian did not know how much time he took. At last, he managed to venture out and put on his clothes.

Lorry waited at the foot of the stairs, arms crossed and foot tapping. She opened her mouth. "We are going to go grocery shopping!" "Why?" Ian blurted. "I thought you always used to complain to me about how I never got the snacks you wanted, right?"

"C'mon, let's go!" Lorry ordered.

They walked to their car, a part sedan and van, and Lorry started the engine. "Buckle up! I have caught you a few times before not having it done!" his mom said.

The ride was 15 minutes long into the suburbs and the car finally parked in the parking lot of Tasty Goods. The parking lot was empty except for a few other cars.

"Mom! This is weird!" Lorry ignored him. "Go get everything you want and bring it back to the shopping cart! Go! Get as much stuff as you like!"

Ian never heard his mom say something like that before. Maybe it was a way to give a message of 'welcome back'.

But there was a huge poster right next to the Tasty Goods sign.

It read: Going out of Business, 50% off of everything inside!

"That is good! Come on, let us buy all we can buy!" Lorry said.

Ian ran into the supermarket and looked for the products he wanted. But just then, he realized the entire vegetable area was empty. Ian went to a different aisle and saw that there were no soft drinks at all.

Ian tried again with the meat and seafood areas. There was no poultry or seafood too! Ian looked around the store to find somebody that could help him. They were the only customers. There was also only two salesmen and he stumbled upon one.

"Yes, what can I do for you?" The salesman sounded bored.

"Where are the ice cream?" "We are out, I'm sorry…" "What about chips?" "Same for them…" "Milk?" "Yup!" "Butter?" "Yup!" "Pastries?" "Yup!" "Fruits?" "Those are the only products we have left." That cannot be!" Then Ian remembered what happened at the Farmlands. He burned everything!

"Where are all the other salesmen and cashiers?" Ian inquired. "They have all resigned," he replied.

"Is this also happening to other stores?" "I am pretty sure."

Then Ian saw his mother running with the cart at him. She reached Ian and halted. "You sir, will explain all this to me! We are leaving," Lorry left the empty cart. She gripped Ian's wrist and pulled him out.

Ian thought of the Tropical Fruit Plantation and instantly understood why there were still fruits. Oh no, Ian thought, I have caused an international issue. "Um mom? May I call Drake, Alexis, Jarret, and Reeve to help me explain?" "No!" Lorry responded.

Chapter Two: The Midnight Raid

Lorry faced Ian. Ian had to face his mom. They sat across from each other. "Take your time, think of a way to explain the cause that led to this effect!"

"Okay, you know the Farmlands? Flix, you have not really met him, but he is a friendly Shadow Clan citizen, noticed poison in the form of a liquid on the crops, so he told us to burn them. It caused a massive wildfire."

"What? You took advice from a Shadow Clan member? Did he go with you and your friends on the trip? I thought Joe was enough for a chaperone! Who needs two?"

"You cannot trust a Shadow Clan citizen, especially when the entire Shadow Clan is under the control of The Haunter already! Where did you guys even meet him? Why didn't you tell me? Now look at what you caused! You people were fooled to do the work of The Haunter! Were you people even sure the liquid was poison? Now where is this Flix? You don't even know! That is the worst part. You were all complete fools!" Lorry fired back.

"Whoa! Calm down first, please!" Ian pleaded and begged.

"He saved me from the Zartees! Without him, we would not have been able to come back alive! He supported us through our journey. I trust him very much," Ian said.

"You were a big idiot!" Lorry cried. "Who would do that?"

"Me?" Ian answered.

"Of course you! But we know that mistakes are mistakes and they cannot be made right again, so we might as well learn lessons from them. But you do not! It all occurred in the past, so now we should just focus on the present and future." Lorry sighed.

"I don't understand why you guys and Joe could seek help from somebody more powerful than you all combined!" Lorry stated. "Well, Flix was an outcast! He believed in helping humans even when the others did not!" Ian told her. "You should have been with us, you would see that Flix was on our side."

"Saving one's life doesn't mean he or she is your friend," Lorry said. "In this case it actually does mean that!" Ian said.

"Besides, Shadow Clan was still governing themselves when we met Flix. The Haunter has not taken over them yet."

"How do you know? Shadow Clan still thinks they are independent! Maybe it was all planned!" Lorry told him.

Ian was not convinced. He trusted Flix with all his heart.

"Fine! You believe what you want to believe. I am a different person, and I know what I believe!" Ian yelled.

"Oh!" Lorry looked disappointed. "Yelling at your mother?"

Ian couldn't take it anymore and he stomped up the stairs to his bedroom, locking the door. His mom always made a big fuss out of something she didn't understand. Ian knew Flix was innocent and his soul was in helping them. My mom will never understand, Ian thought. A few hours later, Ian heard the sound of a doorbell ringing, and then familiar voices. Ian rushed to meet his friends, and cousin. But when he reached the door, Ian stopped for a moment and was afraid his mother would embarrass him in front of them. He had rather not be present physically.

A few minutes later, there was knocking on his bedroom door. He couldn't make out whose it was.

"What? I am not feeling so good and well!" Ian made an excuse. "Open the door! It is me…Drake! My mom said I could come to your house to have a sleepover!"

Ian sat up with excitement and cried, "Really? Is that true?" "Yes," Drake answered swiftly. Ian finally opened the door and to his surprise, Blake the Moygeri was on Drake's back. "You brought him! I thought he was dropped off at the animal shelter!" Ian exclaimed. "Well, he couldn't leave me, and he was just too cute to leave, so yeah!" Drake replied. "Who else is with you?" Ian asked. "Oh, nobody else but me," Drake answered. "What about Alexis?" Ian asked. "She said she couldn't come, but she wouldn't tell me why," Drake responded. At that point, Ian felt like he hit rock-bottom, and the sleepover wasn't as half as exciting as before.

"Um, I only have one queen size and two twin size beds in here that happen to be bunk beds. So do you think we can all cramp inside my room? Are do you want to camp-out in the basement? That will be fun!" Ian said.

"Dude, you make the decision," Drake pointed out. "It is your house! Right?"

"Hey! Let me see your glaive! I have not seen it in millennia!" Ian requested. "It is very cool!" Ian commented at the sight of the silver on each side of the pole.

"Wait, Reeve has a weapon too, but it is close combat. How come she never uses it? A gauntlet?" Ian asked Drake. "Why ask me when I don't know? It is pretty unique anyway," Drake complimented. "I mean, yours is the best of the best!" Drake admired the Wrist Striker 280 on Ian's wrist that could not be taken off. "Yeah, I have grown to like it very much," Ian said. "Let us go down!"

That is what best friends do. They always admire each other's talents, works, masterpieces, or even junk.

Ian hurried down two flights of stairs and got the tent out from the storage. He pumped it up and it rose.

When they were done setting up, they decided to play basketball on Ian's driveway first. "I start, one on one," Ian called. "Put Blake in the baby crib with a few toys, that will keep him occupied," Ian said.

"You sure?" Drake asked reluctantly. "Yes, I think so," Ian assured him. "Don't double dribble!"

"Got it! I never do! Oh, and hey, don't travel, I know you always do that!" Drake retorted, grinning.

"I haven't played for a long time, so take it easy on me!" Ian exclaimed. "I have forgotten all my skills!" Ian dribbled the ball with his left hand and switched a few times.

He dribbled it through his legs and behind his back. Ian tried a jump-shot near the free-throw line but it went off the rim.

Now Drake was in possession. He drove to the basket and made a layup. "See?" Ian said. "Don't be too sure, points up to twenty, okay?" Drake said.

Ian put his body between the ball and Drake and he tried a spin-move, then a shot. The ball flew at the backboard but bounced off the side. Drake took back the ball to the front and crossed-up Ian so bad that he tripped.

Drake did a floater and it went into the basket. 4-0 now.

Ian snatched the ball and rolled it between Drake's legs. Ian went around his foot and picked it up. He attempted a shot right away. It was way off, in fact, an air-ball.

The basketball rolled out of bounce. Drake scrambled to get it back. He stepped into the driveway and they resumed.

Drake got hold of the ball and came in with so much momentum that Ian backed-off and let him take a side-shot.

It went in and made the *swish* sound. "Oh! Nothing but net!" Drake exclaimed. Ian had to try hard now.

Double effort, triple effort. Quadruple effort.

Ian faked a shot, faked a move, and then jumped at the basket. He went straight up, but then Drake smacked and slapped the ball out of his hand.

Ian rebounded the ball and took it back. He took it slow this time.

Ian attempted a fade-away. The ball flew, spinning, and it hit the net, going through it. "Yes!" Ian cried.

"There you go!" Drake said.

After another several rounds, Ian launched the ball. It looked like it went through the basket for the first half-of-a-second. But then, it bounced forward and backwards, hitting the rim a few times, and it flew out.

"No way!" Ian shouted.

"Ha!" Drake exclaimed. "Try again, you still have many opportunities and chances to catch up to me and beat me, but I doubt it, to be candid with you," he pointed out.

The game went on.

Finally, it was 18-17, Drake leading, Ian shot from way downtown and it flew up, curved and arched, straight through the net. Ian had won with a final 3-point shot.

"Oh yeah! I did it! I cannot believe what I just did! How could I win over you? I mean, Drake, you are the pro, not me. In fact, I am the opposite of you!" Ian said.

"Well played anyway! Good game!" Drake responded. They clapped their hands to show good sportsmanship.

"Let's go back inside and play videogames. I am in the mood of it," Ian suggested. "Sure, let's do that!" Drake replied.

"So, what type of game consoles do you have?" Drake inquired as they walked through the front door.

"I have X-box one, X-box 360, PlayStation 1, PlayStation 2, PlayStation 3, and a Wii U. I use only the newest versions," Ian answered. Drake looked amazed. "Wow! You are rich! Where do you even put all this?" "Under the TV," Ian replied like it was obvious.

"What about you?" Ian questioned. "Me? Just Nintendo," Drake responded. "Is that not enough?" he asked.

"Are you satisfied? That is the important thing…" Ian asked.

"I guess so," Drake replied.

So after Ian crushed Drake in videogames, they headed downstairs. Blake caused a big mess that they had to clean up. "I told you that we should have not let him stay down here by himself!" Drake exclaimed. "You never told me in words!" Ian retorted. After cleaning up, they were already very tired, but a night is to cherish and savor, right? They ended up making another big mess with Nerf bullets flying everywhere and hitting every part of the basement.

"Boys!" Lorry cried from the head of the stairs. "It is getting dark! Go to sleep!" They got into the tent.

"There is a sleeping mattress with cushion and one that is air inflatable. Pick which one you want," Ian told Drake. When Drake couldn't decide, Ian picked the air inflatable for him because he was the guest. "Just saying, the air inflatable is less comfy than the one that is now mines for the night."

They started listening to music.

It was about 11:30am when they finally fell asleep. It felt only like 5 minutes until he was woken up by his mom.

"What are you doing?" Ian cried. Drake immediately woke too. Lorry looked apprehensive. "C'mon, follow me," she said.

The two boys followed her up the stairs and to the kitchen. Lorry pointed at the window. "You see that light? They are coming for us! Lock and load! We have to fight for our lives!" she spoke. "Why? What is that?" Drake questioned. "It is them, the evil ones, c'mon, grab a weapon!" "What do you mean? Are you playing with us?" Ian inquired. "The Haunter's minions!" Ian felt a sudden pang of fear.

"Why can't we just run for our lives?" Ian asked. "You think it is that easy? Now, defend the house!" Lorry ordered.

"Can we hide?" Ian inquired. "No! That is the worst thing you can possibly do! They will search every corner of the house because they are determined to kill you, my son!" Lorry screamed. Ian had never heard his mom call him 'son'. He knew this was serious.

Lorry opened the kitchen cabinet and took out a long shotgun.

"Let's rock and roll!" she cried.

Something that sounded like an explosion rocked the house, and the front door blew open. Ian peered around the wall and saw about 30 Dark Elves, Zartees, Sloogpaps, some humans that Ian thought were Moods X Happs, and possibly Ziknios walking, running, and slithering across their lawn.

"They are coming from behind too! And also the sides!" Lorry yelled. "The front, for now at least, is our main concern…"

Drake hid behind the kitchen island, waiting for the stampede.

Ian set his hand on the countertop.

He fired a few bolts of fire through the French doors leading to the patio and porch, cracking the glass.

A gun from the enemy rang and the lamp hanging from the ceiling plunged onto the dining table.

Lorry took the butt of her shotgun and broke the kitchen window. She turned it back around and aimed.

"Drake! Mom! I am going to the living room!" Ian ran past the front door and slid behind a couch. He glimpsed around the sofa and saw assault rifles raised outside. "Oof!" Ian thrusted his head back and he could hear the bullets hitting the carpet and furniture.

After the firing ended, Ian stood 3 quarters up, pressed an unfamiliar button and the Wrist Striker emitted a purplish-white bolt of something that hit a Zartee right in the left eye. He fell backwards. Ian crawled towards the wall, and stationed himself next to two windows. A ladder was put on the bottom of the window because Ian's house was on sort of a little hill. He stretched out his foot and kicked it. The ladder fell sideways, and he could hear pain.

A dark elf climbed into the living room from the other window and Ian was forced to punch him because he did not have any time to shoot him instead.

The dark elf fell out. Ian turned to face the window, shuffled sideways as he fired downwards and took his place at the wall on the other side of where he had been. It was very daring with his entire front exposed to the enemy.

By now, the minions knew where Ian was, and a second sail of gunfire broke out. Ian ducked his head and body.

The bullets penetrated the wall above his head and one by one, they fell onto the carpet. Ian left his place and ran to take cover on a sofa that was large enough to accommodate his entire body when lying down.

There was an arm rest on both sides and one kept Ian's head shielded.

When the coast was clear, Ian lifted his head, brandished his Wrist Striker and started shooting out fire bolts (which was like the original element, according to Ian).

Random people in the crowd were shot and dropped to the ground.

For the first time in Ian's life, he experienced how it was to be in war. It was a lot of stress.

Ian had to take-off his aim and shoot across the living room to take-down others. It was one against many. They kept coming. There were too many of them.

Ian gave up on his shooting and he started having to fight with his wrist. He hit people with the top, swept them away with the bottom, and knocked them unconscious with its side. His hand felt powerful.

But as always, people tend to get tired and weary. In fact, it was the middle of the night. Ian retreated to the kitchen.

Drake fought with all his might as he tried his best to cut-down people. Ian ran to assist him. Drake swung his glaive around and around like he was some master.

Lorry had abandoned her position at the kitchen window and started shooting and reloading continuously. She shot whoever went near her and they all fell at her feet.

The three of them were losing energy.

Finally, the last straw arrived. Thin long cans were thrown into the house. One landed not far from Ian. They emitted green gas that Ian could only think was deadly.

"Out! We have lost! Out!" Lorry screamed. Ian and Drake ran for the back door to the sunroom where home-grown flowers, the mower, and equipment were.

"Ow!" Drake tumbled to the floor. Ian turned to help his friend. He saw that a bullet had flown into the bottom half of the back of Drake's leg. Ian was stunned. Ian lifted Drake unto his shoulders and hauled him out the back door. He desperately dragged him.

Ian limped to the nearest tree and let go of Drake onto the grass. What was he going to do now? "Mom!" Ian yelled. "Mom!" he repeated. At that moment, the entire roof of the house crumbled and a sinkhole opened up, swallowing the house. Ian could not believe his eyes.

I am dreaming, Ian thought.

A Zartee pointed at Ian and the rest of the minions rushed at him.

"Drake! Can you still run?" Ian shook him. "Leave me here," Drake answered. "Please, save yourself," Drake said.

"No, no I can't, I just can't!" Ian cried, his eyes watering. "Trust me…" Drake told him. Ian lied prostrate under the tree.

"Best friends cannot live without each other," Ian said. "We both die!" he concluded and confirmed.

"Ian! Take Drake and go!" came a voice. Reeve and Alexis stood above them. "Get up, we will cover you guys. C'mon!"

Ian would thank them one day for being there. He wasted no time and took Drake on his back.

He ran out of the property and through the woods. Ian ran.

At last, he stopped. Alexis and Reeve caught up with them. "I am pretty sure they lost us already, Alexis' army of deer method worked pretty well," Reeve said. "Oh! And guys, I got a bow and arrows from the sport store!" she exclaimed happily. "Now I have a legit weapon!"

"How did you…?" Ian started. "We knew that Drake had a sleepover with you, so we decided to check out the night at your house. But we became really suspicious when we heard much rustling in the woods and seeing The Haunter's minions again," Reeve explained.

"Um, guys, I didn't mean to disrupt your conversation but look," Drake pointed to the west where there was a good view of Yart.

The whole city was in flames. The skyscrapers looked as if they had certain parts torn off. Steam engulfed the entire city. The buildings all crumbled straight down.

The night of destruction had come. Yart was gone and destroyed. The Haunter's domination process had started.

Ian sat down, putting his hands on his eyes. It was too much. He tried not to weep but felt his eyes water anyway. Drake lied on his good side, dazed. Reeve just leaned against a tree without a word.

Ian took off his shirt and tied it around Drake's wound to stop blood from flowing out. "Are you okay?" "Yes," Drake answered softly. "We will take you to the hospital soon," Ian assured him.

"But right now, for now, I would never have dreamed this would occur one day," Ian choked. Ian was transformed. I will fight for the world, Ian thought angrily. His emotions were mixed. He felt like he had been through too much that was out of his control. He wanted to act tough in front of his friends, but the truth had to be shown. Ian couldn't remember what happened next. Was he still conscious?

Chapter Three: The Wrist Striker 280

Early the next morning, Ian found himself lying prostrate on the forest floor, on a bed of leaves. It was officially autumn. Usually, he would be afraid of ants crawling all over his body, but at this time, it wasn't much of a concern. Ian felt better after a good night sleep, but had not forgotten the horror yesterday.

Ian heard the birds sing to each other for a while. "Finally! About time! I found you all!" came an extremely familiar voice. Ian bolted up and saw his mother.

"Mom! I thought you were dead!" Ian exclaimed happily. "What? Oh yeah, you always wish me the worst," Lorry said sarcastically. "I am so happy to see you lot alive! How desperate was I, and leaving no part of the forest unsearched? It took me forever to get here!"

"By the way," Reeve asked, "How did you even get away from them? I think you know what I'm talking about…" "Oh! Easy-peasy, girl! I hid in the tree until they all left. You know, I am more swift-acting than any of you," Lorry bragged. Reeve turned away. "We need to take Drake to the hospital, he will need medical treatments," Alexis pointed out. "All right," Lorry replied.

"Anybody have a map that can tell us the way out?" Lorry inquired. "I guess not," she sighed. "We shall use our instincts and smell our way out!" she cried.

"Uh, human noses are not that complex or good as dogs," Ian told her. "I am older than all of you, so do whatever I tell you to do!" Lorry quickly fired back.

They groaned.

"Hey, what about I spawn a bubble from my Wrist Striker and it can take you wherever you want to go?" Ian suggested. "Yes!" Lorry answered.

There were a total of 9 buttons and Ian pressed the right one of the top row. Out came something like a blue orb. Drake stood up, winced, and went into it. Lorry followed. The bubble rose gradually.

"We will meet you later!" Ian cried. "The more people inside, the slower it will go!" Ian lied. "Ian! That's not true," Alexis pointed out. "I know, I did that on purpose because I wanted to test every single button on the plate of my Wrist Striker. I can only do it here. If the testing was done in the city or suburbs, the media will get curious and we will be famous…"

"But it's destroyed!" Alexis replied. "Oh, yeah," Ian said, downcast.

"Okay, left to right, all the way down," Ian said. "Sure," Alexis responded. "Um, I will be at the side looking at these leaves," Reeve notified them.

Alexis stood back as Ian hit the first one. Ian aimed it at a tree and out came a bolt of laser. It poked a hole through the trunk of the tree and went out the other side.

"Whoa! Awesome!" Ian exclaimed. Alexis was amazed. "Keep going! I want to see more!" Alexis cried, not even considering the danger that unknown buttons can pose.

Ian clicked the middle one, and out came a bolt of fire that erupted the entire tree in flames. "Ah!" Reeve hurried over and started fanning the flames with a few leaves, extinguishing the sparked fire.

"Next time, you do it yourself!" Reeve announced. "Now, where were we?" Ian asked Alexis. "We know what the next one does…the bubble, so now we continue to the middle row," she said. Ian pressed the left button an out came a white transparent force field. "This can help me to block hits and shield me!"

"C'mon, let's go!" Alexis urged.

Ian went to the next and did the same. But this time, on accident, he pointed his Wrist Striker in the direction of Alexis. Some force wave was emitted and Alexis was blown a few feet backwards.

Seeing this, Ian hurried to her to see if there were any injuries. She was fine, but Ian was shocked. He was not going to do that again when Alexis said angrily, "Do not, do that, ever again, when I'm around!"

"Well, it is my favorite button, and it is pretty fun! I will call it the push-back!" Ian joked. Alexis looked at him like she was serious. Ian stopped and looked at the ground.

After several moments, Ian said, "On to the next one, then!"

He pressed the right button of the middle row and aimed his weapon at a different tree. The tree disintegrated. Reeve ran over and punched Ian hard in the face.

"Why are you killing nature? That was a gruesome way for the tree to die! Why did it deserve that?" "I didn't mean to," Ian cried frantically. That caused him another blow. Alexis jogged over and separated them.

"Reeve! Go back to doing your own business!" Alexis cried. "Ian, resume your testing, there are still 3 more buttons left."

Ian took a deep breath and pressed the first of the bottom row. A plasma orb grew out of the gap in the front of the Wrist Striker and finally detached itself, flying straight at the tree in front of Ian. The process happened before Ian's eyes in a millisecond. The tree appeared as if it was just struck by lightning.

Again, Reeve looked like she was about to beat the life out of Ian. Alexis went to make sure she didn't. They exchanged a few words as Ian just stood there. Finally, Alexis signaled him to continue.

Ian pressed the middle button of the bottom row and out came two curved spikes that retracted from the sides.

"Nice for close-combat!" Ian said. He started moving around and swinging his hand through the air as if he was fighting with somebody.

"Let's move on! The last one!" Alexis rushed him.

Ian pressed it and out came a purplish-white bolt Ian saw yesterday.

He didn't know what it was, but assumed it harmed people as well as himself. "All right! All done!" Ian said.

"Let's go see Drake!" Ian called. He spawned another blue orb and the three of them entered it.

Ian told it where they wanted to go and it took them to the edge of the forest, the outskirts of what used to be the suburbs.

Chapter Four: The Argument

There was a camp there with white tents pitched and a sign reading, 'hospital' since the real one was gone. The bubble popped when it hit the ground and Ian spotted his mom.

"He's inside," Lorry pointed.

Ian opened the flap of the tent and walked in. Drake was sitting on a cot with wheels attached to it on the bottom. He was wearing his regular clothes still.

"They have put some ointment on the wound," Drake said. "Good. I just want to know if you are okay," Ian asked.

"Yes," Drake paused, "Ian, I really liked what you said yesterday about how best friends cannot live without each other, it touched me a lot!" he commented.

"Well, it was from the bottom of my heart," Ian answered. "Was it true that you were willing to die with me?" Drake questioned. "You saw me last night, you make the judgement..." Ian responded. Drake lay back. "I just want to tell you that we are friends no matter what we go through together or if we have any disagreements," Drake said.

"Well, you can count on me to remember that!" Ian assured him. "I've got your back!" "Um, I don't think boys usually talk so emotionally!" Reeve pointed out in a girl-like manner. "Why, we are humans too!" Ian complained.

The doctor walked in and told them to get out so Drake could relax and recover in peace. Ian tried to argue that having himself there helped the patient, but the doctor was not convinced at all. "Patients tend to get better quickly privately when no one is around," the doc pointed out like he was a PHD graduate, which was true. "Um, he actually has a special condition where he likes having me there instead of nobody," Ian retorted.

Tents were set-up on the outskirts of the suburbs, creating refugee camps. The rubble from the main city was in a big mess. Yart was a perfectly beautiful metropolitan area now reduced to ashes.

But in all things, the take-down of Yart was an incident in the past, and Ian should not be sad and thinking about it very much. It would be unhealthy to. Ian's eyes bulged when he saw somebody striding towards him in big steps, and his eyes quickly darted and glanced away. Ian tried to find a place to hide.

It was no other than his old friend Josh, who was, to refresh your memory, the elusive bully and most notorious of all time.

Oh no, I need to get out of here! Ian thought. He went in a circle at where he was, trying to spot anywhere to take cover and shelter. Please, Ian thought. He was in fact at least a tad afraid of Josh, or maybe more. Could he act tough enough to face Josh in a man-like manner? After all, courtesy was the number one key.

"Lanterncup! I thought we would not ever see each other again, which disappointed me! I was very happy to have you in my company, but when you left to go into the world and play, we missed you a great deal!" Josh called out. Josh was a bully who was in fact pretty smart, at least above average, over his buds. "Here is the deal, I will not be mean to you ever again as long as you treat me like a normal person…"

Ian knew better than to accept the deal. He remembered when Josh gave him an 'atomic wedgie' after lunch outside the cafeteria, where there were no teachers or grown-ups watching. It was a painful experience, and very embarrassing. He would never forget it because it was imprinted into his brain. So Ian tried to talk it through. "What brings you here?" Ian gritted his teeth.

43

"Oh…I just wanted to say hi! You know, our school is still standing. But we are forced to evacuate the suburbs to here…and continue our school day here. "But why?" Ian inquired. "We had to take our morning class in an abandoned small building."

"No, I mean…how come you had to continue school?" Ian asked. "Beatrice, our math teacher, told us the *new* principal thought we were lagging and very behind the international education level. I wished Mr. Boris was still here. With him, school was as easy as slicing cheese," Josh informed him.

This was the first time in Ian's life where Josh was actually having a decent conversation with him.

"The truth is…I really want to join you guys," Josh concluded.

Ian's mind almost tore itself apart. "What?" That was none other than his immediate reaction. Why would a former bully who thought he was superior over everybody else now ask to be part of their group? Instead, it should rather be vice-versa! Impossible!

"You have got to be kidding me," Ian told him. "No! I mean it. It might sound crazy, but I want to do something heroic. You see, I knew there is something going on out there when you were all gone. Please let me be part of it. I promise, give me one last chance!"

"Rejected and denied!" Ian quickly reproached, and turned away. "It is extremely dangerous, and the odds of surviving are very low. You should be grateful you were here the whole time! This is serious!"

"Then, how did you all come back in one piece? I can deal with those stuff. I am a bully!" Josh admitted.

"Fine, if you were in our group, what would be the first thing you do, huh?" Ian challenged. "I-I would, um, uh, tell the government about this?" Josh answered earnestly, not sounding too confident.

"Look, the world has just experienced an attack on an entire city, and they were successful at bringing it down!" Ian remarked. "Josh, you are completely out of your mind!"

"That is the bottom line, as well as the headline..." Ian explained.

"You don't have any experience, and you don't even know how it feels like. I am happy to be home. But because of what happened last night, my happiness has faded. Besides, you always go against any of my decisions and actions in school!"

Ian was determined to keep him out.

"I will never be comfortable working with you, and you and I both know that. We are never on the same track. We have different opinions and we work differently. I am saying all this for your sake," Ian said.

"Then, why can you save the world, not me? What is trying to conquer the world anyway?" Josh questioned.

"You don't quite understand, right? This is not something to play with, and is certainly not a game at all," Ian cried.

The conversation wasn't decent anymore. It was getting fiery. "Why don't you find your gang and pretend to save the world yourselves? After everything you have done to me...I know better than to trust you and acknowledge you as a friend!" Ian spat out. Josh put both his hands on Ian's shoulder and pushed him with tremendous force. Ian stumbled back, almost tripping and falling onto his back.

"Lanterncup! I will *kill* you!"

"OH! Physical force? That will never change my mind and view of you, Josh! When have we ever got along?" Ian screamed. "You let me become a member, and the past shall pass," Josh told him calmly.

"Look, I have felt a pang of distress after what happened to both of our homes. My condominium fell before my eyes! That is why I want to do something about it. I want to avenge all those killed here. I miss Yart. I miss the ambience of it. My emotions are mixed! Now, have I said enough? Is it adequate? I feel you too. I have let go of my bad-reputational past. I am not the same as in the past. I have changed, and been transformed. I am not that bad anymore!" Josh delivered out with a strong voice.

Ian's shoulders and muscles relaxed. His anger subsided. "Come here…" Ian went to Josh and hugged him. "I will forget the past. Congrats on getting into the Crystal-Recovered Squad.

You are now officially a member, and of course, my very dear friend!" Ian said. When Ian straightened up, people were crowding around in a circle and watching them with round eyes.

"Oh, okay. Go back to your business, everybody!" Ian ordered.

"Now, can you tell me about what is wrong with the world, and who is the villain?" Josh asked innocently.

Just then, a couple of Josh's old buddies came behind him and stomped up to him and demanded, "What is going on? We watched the entire showdown. The rest of us have decided that we want to overthrow you and elect a new leader…" "You cannot or I will kick you out and make you pay for your disobedience and insubordination!" Josh fired back. The gang instantly lost its courage and turned their backs to walk away.

"What I meant there was…I will not see or meet them ever again. But I will contact them, but after this is all over, whatever it would be," Josh assured Ian.

"Hey!" Ian and Josh sprang. Drake was on crutches.

"Good news, I didn't lose my leg!" "Well, that is only the least of things that go our way," Ian remarked.

"C'mon, we have a new recruit, and he will be very useful to us. We have much work to do." "Why is he here?" Drake questioned. "No time to explain. It might seem awkward, but you will get it later. Tell Alexis, Reeve, Jarret, and my mom to come," Ian told him.

Chapter Five: The Voting & Discussion

"Today, September 1st, Josh Heartbee has become one of us and will permanently be…" Ian announced.

"Ian! Are you crazy?" they all said at once. "Just what I've expected. I will explain, but no complaints or disruption while I talk, good?" Ian asked.

They all eyed Josh as if he was Lucifer the Devil or something.

Ian had led them somewhere quiet and made sure there weren't in fact any eavesdroppers who lived upon the action.

"Josh has shown me that he is eligible for this job. That is all you people need to know. Done. Over!"

"How can it be? Is this some kind of bribery or something? And in that case, you are very corrupt!" Alexis brought up.

Ian stopped in his tracks.

"Have faith in me! Do not worry. He is our colleague now!" Ian responded. "Well, there is a difference between a good one and a bad…" Reeve trailed off.

"Ian, this is unacceptable. Get him away! How much have you told him about us yet? Please don't say it is a lot," Lorry pleaded. "In fact, I haven't told him a single thing yet, that is why he is so curious!" Ian replied.

"You may all see Josh as a very nasty and immature person, but you know, after the tragedy of Yart, he has switched roles. Josh wants to help the world now!"

Josh nodded his head in approval as Ian presented him with his hands. Nobody clapped or showed any sign of agreement. They all seemed concerned about all this.

"But how are you sure?" Lorry shot out. "I am not," Ian admitted, "But I trust him after his testimony."

Lorry opened her mouth so wide as if she couldn't believe her own son and his very unwise decision. "Ian, you are not the kid I know. May you please send that extremely immodest kid away?"

"No!" Ian slipped out of the gap between his lips. Lorry let out a quick loose of air. "I am the leader, remember guys? Joe made me the new leader!" Ian said.

"I knew it. One day, my son will make decisions that will bring him shame rather than success and he will regret it. That day has come. You know what, Ian Lanterncup? I am your mother, take that!" Lorry cried.

Drake and Jarret started making 'burn' and 'roast' noises. Even Blake was trying to do them by watching.

Ian was about to fire back when Alexis broke in. "Let us stop this nonsense. This is a waste of time and it is not helping us whatsoever," she commented.

"I say we do a vote. What about that? Majority rules," Alexis suggested. Everyone nodded.

"It would be fairer and also avoiding belligerent people yelling at each other's faces and condescending their dignities. Let us start the process now."

"Those who want Josh in, say "I"," Alexis exclaimed. Ian said "I". Jarret said "I", and Drake said "I". Ian was surprised that the other two boys were fine with Josh. He just needed one girl/women vote to win, or else there would be a gender gap. C'mon, just one more, Ian thought. Please?

Alexis and Reeve both decided to raise their hands in favor. "What?" Lorry shouted. "Why? I am out!" Lorry threatened.

"Mom! You will not affect us if you leave," Ian pointed out.

She seemed to be hesitating because she kept changing her mind and going back and forth. "Fine! I lose to a group of kids. I will stay just to protect you guys that is all..." Lorry finalized and concluded.

"All right, let us say hello to our new comrade!" Ian started applauding and the rest followed.

"Thank you for all those who voted for Josh. Thank you!" he repeated.

"He shall give a speech now," Ian announced. The spotlight went on Josh even though only less than 10 people were watching, and one animal.

"I will never let you down, like a presidential nominee that is it. My speech is over," Josh said. "No way! That was short!" Ian exclaimed. "Sorry, I am not a good public speaker, forgive me. But I already go the main point out," Josh answered.

"Uh, Ian?" Josh grinned. "I do not know who those two are," pointing to Reeve and Jarret. "Man, she is *hot!*"

Josh was a guy who was very open with his feelings and never kept it in. Ian guarded his with maximum security. Ian kept his mouth shut, not knowing what to say.

They spent the next hour telling Josh about what was going on in the world and what happened during their very journeys. They filled him up with information.

"I have been missing so much! Sounds fun!" Josh answered sarcastically at the end. "But I know our tasks are huge."

"Everything you have told me is unbelievable. But I believe you," Josh told them. "I truly do."

"So, what do we do first?" Josh asked. "What was that plan of yours, besides?" Ian returned.

Josh grinned. "We are heading south to the capital of our continent. Tapwa is our next destination."

Chapter Six: A New Friend

For the majority of the day, the Crystal Recovered Squad weren't too fond of Josh. Even Ian had some difficulty and his own doubts about Josh. Josh would most likely be a big burden to the team. He was not qualified.

On the other hand, Ian felt like the environment was different somehow…with Josh and his sudden transformation. He knew he was judging Josh too much and wondered if his assimilation was a good choice made by himself and the others.

Ian tried to set aside the negative thoughts of Josh. His number one worry was that Josh was putting on an act and this was not his true self. Maybe he was working with them to earn back glory?

Ian believed he needed to trust his decisions because they were made already. It didn't really go well with himself being extremely reluctant about this one.

Was Josh going to benefit or harm them? Ian always repeated the same cliché to himself. It is: "Go with your instincts."

Ian just couldn't. It felt like his soul was raging war on itself. His body was like in a civil war, tearing itself apart.

But what Ian worried the most was how his friends felt and thought about what he created. Ian was afraid that he had let the team down. Had he done his crew a favor or not?

Ian knew not to let fear govern his body. All this came down into one question. It was: "Did I do the right thing?"

He feared much not.

"Ian! Come on! We are going!" Drake shouted. Ian fell awake. He had been daydreaming while sitting on a bench.

They were at a train station 5 miles from the city of Yart.

Alexis had recommended for them to all take a train. Since there weren't any more transportation options, Ian agreed almost immediately. The train was delayed, but it got to the station at somewhere in the middle of 3pm to 4pm. The passengers started walking onboard. "You are all lucky that I have Benjamins!" Lorry stated.

"I grabbed my wallet before our house was taken over!" she cried. "It was because of me that we bought our tickets!"

"Yeah, yeah," Ian slipped out. Ian knew it was true, but he didn't want his mom to have an advantage over them.

It was like a plane but on the ground. The train finally started moving. Nobody spoke a word to Josh.

Josh kept his eyes staring out, through the window. It was very unusual because Ian once knew him as a kid who was very loquacious. He couldn't stop.

He watched different landscapes fly by. Ian felt bad for him, truly.

Ian never dreamed of knowing Josh as an outcast who couldn't fit in. He was opposite from what he was before.

Reeve went to Lorry and asked her, "Can we go see if there are any good food?" Lorry approved, and Drake and Alexis followed her away.

Ian took a step of faith and tapped Josh's shoulder. He turned his head. "What?" Josh moaned.

"You will be forever my friend," Ian choked. Somebody clapped in the seat behind Ian's. "Well said," Jarret informed him. Ian was sitting next to Josh.

Prior, when they had to choose seats, Ian just went to sit with Josh. His friends had given him evil-eyes. Ian had tried not to show his weakness. It was hard, but he was indeed successful.

"Jarret! Why didn't you go with them? I thought you left! And mom! Were you listening?" Ian cried.

There was no word from his mom, but Jarret spoke up. "I just wanted to be with you two, because I am your caring cousin," he said. Josh lifted his head.

"Thank you…"

Ian smiled. This was repairing wounds.

10 minutes later, the rest of the Crystal Recovered Squad returned, and asked Ian's mom for 100 bucks total.

Lorry sprang in her seat. "Are you kidding me? Do I look rich to you? I already payed for all those tickets! Why can't you guys share instead? Is the food that expensive?"

"Unfortunately, yes," Alexis grinned unconvincingly. Her grin faded and they stared at the ground glumly. "But I'm hungry!" Drake gave a shot at it.

"You know what? Go call your own mama and tell her to come pay for it herself…!" Lorry fired back.

Ian could not stand it. Why was his mom being so nasty?

He stood up and looked right smack into her eyes and spoke, "Give them what they need!" Ian sat back down.

Lorry muttered something but didn't argue back somehow. She took out a Benjamin and gave it to Reeve.

"It's yours, don't think of giving it back to me. It is officially yours!" Lorry warned. Alexis made eye-contact with Ian and she looked very dumbfounded.

For the rest of the way, Lorry was soundly asleep, dwelling in her own dreams. Ian was happy that his mom was asleep and not causing any trouble. In his mind, his mother was the most annoying person in the whole wide world. He couldn't stand her.

She was always raising her voice. His dad on the other hand was the calmest guy in the world. How did they even fall in love? Ian knew he wouldn't be there if not, so he must be thankful. Other than what just happened, the entire trip was pretty peaceful and calm. Nobody said a word.

Well, maybe there were whispers, but there was not much socializing and association going on. Everybody was in their own worlds. Ian was in his, thinking about nonsense.

At last, and finally, the train halted. Everyone got up and scrambled to take their things.

There were a lot of displaced people onboard from Yart, some of which Ian thought looked familiar.

As you can guess, not much luggage or belongings.

Then, the typical announcement was spoken where there was a 'thank you' and 'please come again and 'it was a pleasure to serve you' short speech by the captain.

The sliding doors opened up, and the Crystal Recovered Squad left the train and went up the escalators into the heart of Tapwa.

It was a big and nice-looking city. Cars honked, entrepreneurs walked the streets, and hobos lay against walls, and middle-class people occupied sidewalks and walking their dogs.

This was the center of daily life. Block after block of apartments and little shops below lay before Ian's eyes.

Then, Ian spotted a place called Defense Store and decided to go there. "Josh, let us get a weapon for you!"

They rushed in and the feeling of AC embraced Ian.

"Walk around, browse, find something you like…" Ian said.

Josh was excited and Ian waited at the front door for him to come back. He did, carrying a small metal gadget.

"What is this?" Ian questioned. "Oh! A Taser of course! And also, this is just the back-up weapon I want. I am planning to get those two automatic rifles. They aren't too long and not too big. They are the perfect size to carry around! See? You see does?" Josh blurted.

"That means taking cash out of my mom's purse again…" Ian moaned.

He went to where everybody else was waiting and asked for the money. Lorry was reluctant, but Alexis urged her to do it with an excuse by saying it was "For the good." Lorry handed over the money and said this was the last time.

Ian nodded and went back. They paid for the weapons and when Josh came out of the dressing room, he looked like he was prepared for war. "Out we go!" he said with pride.

When he walked out, Reeve exclaimed, "Wow!" She stepped over to Josh and admired him. Josh looked as if he was very proud of himself for getting the weapons AND the lady. Josh had both his guns on either side of his waist, attached to a belt.

Where was the Taser, anyway?

"How much change is there? Was there a discount? If so, how much percentage? Please tell me! By the way, I thought you needed a license to buy high-class weapons like those," Lorry nudged. "The law is not valid here," Josh explained. "That is why…"

Josh didn't answer any of the other questions. "Besides! I am carrying a glaive!" Drake broke in.

"Uh, Josh? You wouldn't be worried that the police will keep a big eye on you with those around?" Jarret asked.

He eyed the guns wearily. "What did you get other than those?" "A Taser!" Drake told him. "Cool!"

"C'mon, the Government Plaza is just a few blocks away, let's go!" Ian exclaimed. They headed in the direction.

The capitol was a massive Victorian style building. It was sitting on a flat piece of land, and a green pasture.

"I guess we should just go knock," Josh recommended.

"No! That is the dumbest thing I have heard from you ever!" Alexis replied. "No way! We are not doing that!"

"I got it. Let's buy a microphone!" Jarret suggested. "Before that, can we go get some food?" Ian broke in. "Hello! I am losing cash out of my account! Fine, because my duty is to feed you, I will pay with credit," Lorry retorted. "No doubts, I help generously…" she continued. "Go pick your restaurant, anyone. It may be fancy or fast, so hurry up before I change my mind! You're lucky I got a raise at my babysitting job a few months ago. Now my earnings are draining away!" Lorry finished. Ian could never imagine his mom being a nanny, and taking care of somebody else's child. She never got a college degree, so it was all for making a living.

Ian almost smiled at this. It was a very ludicrous thought. He wondered how the baby or toddler had felt.

"Look! A pho!" Drake exclaimed. "What is that?" Reeve asked him. "You never heard of them? Beef noodle soup, they are amazing! Also, I will most likely order the crispy roll too, my stomach needs it. My taste buds are craving right now," Josh explained. "Come, I will introduce you!"

Whatever Josh said, Reeve agreed. There was some sort of telepathy between them and going on currently.

"I'm full, you guys go!" Alexis told them. Jarret and Lorry followed Ian. Ian knew they were hungry.

"We are coming along too! Don't forget us!" Josh exclaimed.

He took Reeve's arm and they walked together as if leaving the stage after a wedding as the bride and groom. Reeve beamed excitedly.

"Hey, I will stay here with Alexis. We will go walk in the park and get some sunshine. Meet here in 45 minutes, okay?" Drake said. They agreed and left the spot. "Don't get lost!" Lorry cried.

"I am sure they will not," Ian retorted. Lorry gradually calmed herself before her anger-meter would reach 100. Ian knew this was happening. "Pho! Here we come!" Jarret called.

They were shown to their table (2) by a kind waitress. Reeve and Josh sat at a two person table like they were on a date. Ian had to share a table with his god-like mom and his rather mysterious cousin.

"May you like to start with beverages? We sell bubble and green tea. They are our daily special starting at just 4.99!" the waitress exclaimed.

They all asked for ice water with lemon and the waitress departed.

"I am so taking the meatball one! It has been a whole year since I was at a Pho. Remember the one near your house, Ian?" Drake asked. Ian was too busy thinking when he finally got back to his senses.

"Yeah, I also know a few other ones, and the funny thing is, they all have numbers after them! I know one is 67, another-22, and…I forgot. It has been so long ago! Can you believe it? Time flies!" Ian replied.

Ian spotted Blake wander through the entrance to the restaurant. He never really did anything but lie on Drake's back all day. He was a pretty unique creature.

The only resource they had was Lorry, Ian knew. She was the only one with cash. Ian was the only one left with his duffel bag, but it contained no monetary value.

Then, Ian thought of Joe. He was the best man he had ever met. His profile didn't fit him. His career of being a janitor totally did not. Ian did not need to feel sad over Joe's death. He had fulfilled his destiny.

The food came in under 5 minutes. Ian was amazed. That fast? Seriously? He took the curved spoon to drink soup and dipped it into the bowl. Ian got some liquid and brought it to his lips. It was steaming hot.

"Ah!" Ian dropped the spoon into the broth and some drops flew into his face, shirt, and pants. Even worse, his elbow hit the glass water and all of it dumped onto his thighs.

Every customer inside was watching him and his reaction. This was extremely embarrassing. He wished he was not there.

This was not good.

Lorry smacked her forehead with her hand and said, "You are not three years old!" Ian got out of his seat and hurried to the bathroom. "Mommy? Is he peeing?" a little boy asked as Ian fast-walked by him.

Ian's cheeks flushed as he slipped into the restrooms and locked the door. Ian gave out a sigh of relief.

"Thank you!"

He washed his face, clothes, and everything else that might have been affected. By the time he was out, he figured his food was already cold and his friends and relatives were gone. But they weren't.

The soup was warm, but not hot, which Ian enjoyed.

He tried using chopsticks and failed a few times, but then mastering the skill after. Ian ate several globs of vermicelli.

Then, Ian started studying Reeve and Josh. He tried to eavesdrop, but it was hard being tables away. They were laughing hard, as Josh bit into his crispy roll. They seemed perfect together. Reeve nested her right cheek on her hand, which appeared *so* attracting.

Her eyes were kept on Josh as she twirled her straw, taking a sip moments later. Reeve looked very innocent. She had a strong charisma, and Ian just could not stand it, in a rather good and positive way.

"What? Dreaming about something?" Lorry patted Ian's back. "This is delicious! I am going to come back again, I tell you!" Jarret told them as he devoured his food.

"Nothing, mom. I am just tired," Ian responded. It was a pretty lame excuse in front of his mom.

"By the way, this food is good stuff!" Jarret interrupted.

Chapter Seven: The Scare

Before long, it was time to go. Lorry payed at the cashier.

Then, Ian heard an angry yelp from his mom and then, "Why is it so expensive? This is a huge rip-off! Are you trying to swindle my money? What is going on?"

"You already ate the food, so," the cashier told her. "Tell me exactly what kind of joke this is or you and I will walk together into court!" Lorry demanded.

"Fine! Look! I am breaking a promise now. The Food Manufacturing Association has told us that there has been a mysterious burning of the farmlands."

"Also, only a portion of the land and livestock are left, everything else consumed by the flames. This makes the world low on food products. Believe it or not, we are about to go into a famine!" the cashier answered.

"How come the news isn't telling us any of this?" Lorry questioned. "Well, the government doesn't want the media to know, and therefore the citizens too, that is why we are charging you more and I am breaking a promise thanks so much to you!" the cashier concluded.

"I mean, they sent emails only to restaurant owners around the world. The thing is, they say they are dealing with this issue right now and we don't have to worry for now. At this chance, they are seizing the opportunity to tax us more, which means taking money from citizens…" the cashier explained.

"The government is doing this? No way. You mean the one in Tarso? Them? They are behind all this? This is cheap! They cannot be doing this! What kind of leadership is this? We are about to enter an international famine?" Lorry was enraged.

This shook everybody in the restaurant. Ian knew the rumor was going to spread quickly. The secret was not going to last.

It really caught the attention of everyone in the room. "I felt like it was right to let the citizens know about this," the cashier acknowledged. "You did the right thing. This problem is severe. We will have to deal with it fast!" Lorry told him. "But fear not! We will get the government working quickly and swiftly!"

"One more thing, you are speaking the truth, right?" Lorry questioned. "Of course? You really believe I am a liar?" "Just checking to be sure, you know…"

"Well, thank you very much. I will be going on my way now. Farewell!" Lorry said to the cashier, slamming the cash onto the counter. Ian, Jarret, Josh, Reeve, and Blake followed her out the door. This was totally unexpected. This was no good.

They found Drake and Alexis and told them everything. "How can this be?" Alexis retorted. "Amazing, absolutely amazing!" Drake responded clearly.

Jarret went to buy a microphone and got back before 2 minutes was up. Lorry had given him 50 bucks, which was enough. "Are you sure about this?" Jarret asked. "I don't know! You tell me!" Drake replied.

"I do not feel like this is right. Wouldn't it be invading their privacy? I feel pretty nervous about what we are about to do—the whole speaking into microphone thing," Alexis brought up. "Oh cheer up, this is nothing! It is so simple," Ian retorted.

The gate doors were left wide open, somehow, like they were welcomed to walk in anytime.

"Bad security," Josh murmured to Drake. "Very true."

Ian took the microphone and marched in and immediately spotted a hill that looked like a good place to stand and speak.

"What are you doing? This is insane! Do you not have common sense?" Lorry suddenly cried. "Why? I thought you agreed to this, right?" Ian asked back.

"I didn't know it would be like this! Come back out! That is a prohibited area! You are trespassing!" Lorry yelled at him.

"What about them? They are flushing in too!" Ian pointed to the rest of them. "No excuses, just trust me! I am your mom!" Lorry responded firmly.

"I don't know about this, I don't feel okay," Reeve told Josh. "C'mon, you have that awesome bow of yours, you can stop anything coming at you!" he replied.

Ian ignored his mom's angry fit and waited for the rest of his companions to catch up. Then, he took the microphone, clicked the on button, played around with it, and tested his voice.

It was loud, so loud that the whole Government Plaza and Square hear his voice. Ian wished he had never tried it. He will not do that ever again.

Plus, Ian made an awkward sound.

"Lemme try it," Jarret snatched it from his hands even though he was so short. He put it into position as Lorry continued to scream at them. Jarret said, "Ladies and gentlemen inside, we want to talk you."

For a second, there was awkward silence. The screaming from Lorry had stopped. She knew she had failed.

"Well at least we tried..." Ian started. There was movement from atop, and then Ian saw two canines rushing at them from the building.

"Oh! Hey doggies!" Ian exclaimed. The canines were very cute with their tongues sticking out and flying through the wind. Their eyes looked very innocent. One headed straight at him. It got so close that Ian thought he was going to pet it and touch it.

"Ruff!" the dog exclaimed and jumped from his hind legs. Ian screamed in astonishment and attempted to shield his body with his arms. The dog tackled him to the ground. Ian started struggling to get out of its grasp as its wet nose kept rubbing against him. The canine's paws dug deep into Ian's belly, causing him to yell in agony. Ian was rather germ phobic.

"Stop it! Stop it! AAGH!"

Out of the corner of his eye while being tossed around on the grass, Ian could see the other canine taking down Ian's friends one-by-one. He wanted to help them.

Soon, police deputies started jogging out with their guns raised.

This was not going to plan at all.

"That kid over there is armed! Get down to your knees!"

"Hey! Arms up right now or I will shoot!" one cop cried.

Josh fell to his knees and lifted his hands slowly. Ian knew the guns strapped to his belt were the signs of harm.

People gathered at the lawn fence to watch the live action.

An officer cried out a command, and the canine grasping Ian released him. Ian breathed out a sigh of relief.

Good experience. "Who is the leader here, huh?" one guy asked.

They all pointed to Ian. "Yes, I am, can we talk inside after I wash-off in the bathroom? Please?" He nodded, and they were escorted through a side door. "We will need to take your weapons, sorry," the cop said. "No problem with me, you mean all of us? That is fine," Ian answered.

Chapter Eight: A Meeting of Officials

The Government Plaza building was gorgeous. Everything was archaic in a good way. Old anything wasn't always bad. Paintings of people in white wigs with curled-hair stood at their spots on the rustic wall. Spiral staircases appeared and disappeared.

Lanterns hung off hooks on little tables everywhere. Ian smirked at the thought of his last name. What ancestor could have come up with the ridiculous name? Fireplaces sat on the floor adjacent to the wall with mantels above them. Old books with dust all over them were on the mantels. Every room was separated from each other. There was no such thing as open-concept there. Marble tiles lay on the floor.

The place was magnificent.

"Hey! This is not a time to be wowed!" A guard walked over and snapped. "We are taking you to the Room of Non-Recreation." "What a name!" Jarret blurted. "It is legit, okay? Don't judge…" the guard returned swiftly. They entered into a modern conference room like the one in the top floor of a skyscraper. Chairs that could roll-around sat side by side along a long table.

Huge windows replaced the wall opposite and the sides.

One of the chairs had its back facing them. It was at the head of the table and was so enormous that Ian didn't know there was a person sitting in the chair.

It spun around and revealed a man with gelled and wavy hair. He was obviously wearing a red tie and black jacket.

His hand went to a phone on the table and he dialed a number. The man spoke a few words into the phone: "What are you waiting for? Get your dirty butts over here! We have business to do! Now!"

Ian's first impression of the guy was a rather negative view.

He didn't like him, of course.

A few two-digit seconds later, couple men entered the room. One had a badge along with a formal nametag that wrote Joint Chief of Staff and made out of plastic. His jacket had many buttons in it and a collar at the neck. The other person was a National Caregiver according to the tag, which Ian never heard off.

The man at the front of the table was none other than the Commander in Chief, which was the President.

"So what seems to be the problem here?" said the President. "Oh!" he corrected after a quarter-second, I forgot to introduce you to my colleagues. "This is Ahmed Bashur Abdullah, the Joint Chief of Staff, and this is Mr. Sammy Sam, the National Caregiver…"

"Yes, there is an issue," started Alexis. "What issue? I can solve it!" the President told her. "We are being threatened by something called The Haunter. It may sound fictional, but it is real. Remember those times when that plane fell down, when there was a massive earthquake at the Mountain of Day and Night, and cities cracking down involving Yart? You know what is causing all this? A spirit from space! We believe he has a massive army about to take over the world, and that involves the Shadow Clan territory. So please, ask all your questions right now. We decided to bring this up to higher authority so we could address it sooner. We need to let you important officials know!"

"Wait a minute? Is this all true anyway? And how do you know? And what kind of clan is this, here to confront us?" the Join Chief of Staff questioned. "Fine, tell them everything! I don't know! I wasn't here the whole time with you guys," Josh suggested.

"Yo! Drake, give them the entire story!" Ian tapped his finger on the table. Drake looked reluctant. "I am serious, I am pretty sure we are doing the right thing," Ian concluded. "Well, it is too late anyway, since you are here and the words have slipped out of your mouths, so um," the National Caregiver told him.

"Just saying, we are the Crystal-Recovered Squad, and Drake will explain that too, go ahead, I'm done!" interrupted Alexis.

Drake went through the story and talked about how Ian's Grandfather Clive a long time ago, fought with the Haunter and weakened him, but now he was back in power. Also, Drake talked about how they got their weapons in a janitor's closest mysteriously, survived ambushes and a plane breaking apart in the air, a hotel breaking apart, a restaurant blowing up, seizing a crystal from dragons, Shadow Clan refusing their gift, everything that happened in between, and everything else.

It took a very long time.

At the end, they were shaking their heads as if they could not believe all this. "This is not a prank, right?" the National Caregiver asked. "Nope! Not at all!"

"We will just have to trust you people," the President confirmed. "I believe you, and I will get to work!"

"Yeah, I've been getting letters from an unknown person saying that I was going down and I should prepare my military fast before I get punched in the face, you know. And they get delivered right to the door!" the Joint Chief of Staff pointed out.

"I think it is time we should get involved after that 'burning of the fields' problem. Do you people know anything about that?" the National Caregiver asked.

"Uh, uh-huh?" Reeve smiled. "Well, a Shadow Clan friend of ours discovered poison on the grain and we decided to burn everything before everybody dies," Ian reported. "We didn't mean any harm..."

"Shadow Clan hates us! You got help from one? Foolish! Oh well, I know people make mistakes, so do not be too disappointed, just don't repeat the same mistake, please. You people have created a worldwide thing that will surely not be over shortly," the President told them. "This is all too hard to take-in."

"So, are there any more questions?" the Joint Chief of Staff asked. "I don't think…" Ian trailed off. "Yes! I remember that there is something about a certain code that we need to crack," Alexis cried.

"What is that?" Ian fired. "You forgot already? Flix told us about this. One of the Four Steps is to crack the Anything Code. But we just don't know where it is and what it is. So, I just wanted to ask…"

Alexis winked.

Ian was going to yell at her, but after experiencing the wink, he settled down and replayed it in his mind. Her wink soothed his nerves.

"They won't know!" Drake announced.

"At least I try, so, you know anything about the Anything Code?"

"Search it up online!" the President said. "On one of our websites!" He took a laptop from a bag that lay next to the leg of his chair. It read Top Secret on it.

"Technology is awesome! You can find anything on it!" "Type www.govnetc.com and you will get information in every area of life," the National Caregiver said.

Ian did and out came a webpage with a search bar at the left. He typed in 'Anything Code' and out came a picture of ice and sky. There weren't any words. Ian looked around and started clicking the background.

Two words came out: North Pole. Ian's mind flashed. "I got it! We need to get there and grab the Anything Code! Thanks Alexis! C'mon, let's go!"

"As you wish, I will be getting on my work now. I even need to cancel my trip to Yun. Well, my job is to keep people satisfied and this continent safe. So, I need to think of an alternative," the President started. A couple seconds passed and, "All right, we shall send our workers to the Tropical Fruit Plantation to store fruit that our citizens will need to live on as we investigate the Farmlands," he finished. "Farewell! Get on your way. Soon, I will learn more about this Haunter guy, or spirit, whatever! Hey Sammy! Go get to spreading the word. And Ahmed? I need you to go to the Cove to tell our generals about this!" the President ordered.

"This meeting is dismissed!" the President pounded the table. The Crystal-Recovered Squad filed out of the conference room and eventually out the main door.

"It is time for the media to understand and we must brace ourselves for whatever response the masses would give!" the National Caregiver said from behind.

They walked peacefully through the lawn and out the gate. The bystanders had disappeared, probably because they took such a long and gruesome time.

"Hey! That went well, I expected total chaos!" Jarret brought up. "They have a lot to do, you know."

"Oh hey! I forgot to return your weapons! They look very nice!" the Joint Chief of Staff came running out. "Wow, I can't believe we forgot to ask you for them! Thank you. Without them, I fear we will not be able to continue with what we are doing," Ian answered. They went on their way. "Dude! If we didn't have our weapons, we are pretty much doomed because I think we are printed on Haunter Times or something…" Drake grinned.

The rest of them laughed, but none knew what was laying ahead.

Chapter Nine: The Retrieving

Lorry found a ferry for tourism going to the North Pole about to take-off and that there were just enough tickets and room left for all of them. So, they went at it.

It left a port with people from all over the world and slowly steamed off north. The trip was supposed to take a few hours.

The water turned icy slowly and glaciers started to appear.

"Oh, why didn't we get a wooly jacket? At least one for me?" Jarret whined, rubbing his arms with his hands by crossing them.

The sky was very cloudy and misty.

Then, Ian recognized permafrost on the ground. The wind started to carry snow around at 70mph. "Huddle! Get to cover! Whose idea was this anyway?" Josh shouted.

It got so bad that Ian couldn't even open his eyes at all. Josh grabbed Ian's arm and the rest of them joined together to conserve human-body heat which Ian suddenly thought was nasty but would rather have it. There were many mini snow-tornadoes that released snow onto every surface of the boat and quickly turned into ice.

"Help! Help!" Drake groaned. Ian was about to say the same, but it would be useless because only somebody insane would travel to the North Pole in an open ferry without indoors. No wonder it was so cheap.

Ian heard the boat hitting islands and chunks of ice. At one time, the boat tilted sideways and Ian just forced himself to hop up to grab onto the other side. He knew some ice had broken off from a tall glacier and fallen onto the edge of the right hand side.

The ferry continued to move-on automatically without a driver. Ian learned a lesson: Only go on a moving thing with a driver on with an exception of roller-coasters and probably waterslides, even though he rarely went to an amusement park.

The business had fooled them into paying for this ride.

He could hear other people yelling at each other and holding on to something tight as the boat ventured through water in the negative degrees. The freezing water was aggressive. He wouldn't want to be in it. Ian heard the ferry crashing into floating ice.

They slowly drifted. The experience was kind of like white water rafting but more severe. Jarret suddenly ran to the edge of the boat and barfed his pho overboard because of tremendous sea sickness. Reeve held her tummy and took deep breaths to calm herself down or maybe tried not to barf too.

Ian could hear his mom regretting the decision from sounds she made. She was snorting and asking herself, "Why?" over and over again like she failed as a guardian/parent of Ian's. Lorry stomped her feet variously and punched the floor and everything.

Ian believed that they were all lying on the ground now as the freezing wind blew around. Ian was always afraid of the floor. It had a lot of germs in it, especially carpet.

"When is this going to end?" Alexis cried. "I know, right?" Josh backed-up. "We just need to get to our destination and get that thing, that code!" Josh yelled.

And then, the weather gradually switched to being serene. It was like entering the eye of a storm. This must be some trick. How could it be? Perfectly nice weather, just a tad cold, but that didn't matter.

"Oh my goodness! Finally!" Reeve cried joyfully. "Are we dead? Is that why?" Drake thought. The sun shone bright and round, but the ice refused to melt.

"Nature is so beautiful!" Alexis exclaimed. "I do agree," Josh replied. "Now, when is this ride going to end? And how long do we get? And where should we go now? And where could it be? I mean really!" Drake asked.

"Well, according to this half-torn-apart brochure I have here, we have about 15 minutes before departure," Ian said.

"What? That is it? That is not enough time!" Drake cried. "I am sorry, but we will need to hurry up anyway…" Ian replied.

"You should have done some research before we went on this ride and gotten ourselves to the North Pole!"

"I refuse to go that way back again. Never in my life will I do that again! No! Even as much as anybody persuades or tries to convince me! No! Never again!" Drake cried. "Then, I think you should…" Ian returned nastily. He was about to say something not very nice and offensive but stopped there because it would hurt a lot.

"Enough! Kids! You are all teenagers! Get mature!" Lorry interrupted, stepping between them. "Live with this! Control your tempers! It is all fine!"

"It is not like you are going to die! Please, I beg you, be flexible! You people need anger management!" Lorry yelled. "Well, one line you said wasn't true. We could have died!" Drake returned.

"Will you please shut up?" Lorry screamed. Drake pursed his lips and looked away, turning his attention.

No one spoke.

The ferry boat hit grassy-ground and people started getting off. More than 50% of the people remained on the boat. Drake refused to get off, so he made a promise that he will stay at the same area no matter what. Ian, Alexis, Reeve, Josh, Jarret, and Lorry got off the ferry and started looking around.

"Here you go, binoculars, Ian! I knew you would need them!" Lorry took one out of his purse.

"Thanks, mom!" Ian put them to his eyes and looked around.

"See anything?" Alexis asked. "Uh…aha! Yes! This way and direction!" Ian exclaimed deliberately. They used up like 5 minutes before stumbling upon an igloo with an unknown flag standing outside.

"Are you sure this is where it is?" Josh questioned. "Not at all! Let's go find out!" Ian responded.

Ian led the group and walked through the mostly-oval door, except the bottom was flat. A feeling of warmth encompassed him. It felt *good.* There was a fire in a hearth standing beside the wall. A circular mat made of goat-skin lay on the floor. And in the center was an old man meditating.

"Welcome! What do you seek from me? I am the one and only Wise Man!" "Oh! Uh! Nothing!" Ian grinned unconvincingly. He really wanted to ask the man how old he was, but he was afraid it would be rude even with a man.

"I can tell you are lying. Why else would you be standing in my igloo with a few other people with what looks to be weapons: guns, sword-like thing, bow-arrows, and some gadget on the wrist? I can tell that you are all searching for something crucial!" the Wise Man spoke steadily.

He had a goatee with the tip touching his waist. He looked very old.

"How do you know all this and be sure from the sound of your voice?" Ian questioned. "How? I can tell from the scenario itself!" the Wise Man called.

"I have experienced life longer than anybody else has. I know when somebody is telling the truth and when they aren't. I can tell what anybody's intentions are by the look of your faces, do you understand? That is why being old is awesome, because you know everything and anything!" the Wise Man said. "I do not believe youngsters like you and that adult of yours understand what the meaning of life is, but I do!" he concluded.

"That is it! We are at the right place! You, the Wise Man, knows everything and *anything*. So, we seek the Anything Code..." Ian revealed. The Wise Man nodded.

His tone changed.

"It was a gift from a friend who I will not reveal his name. The Anything Code is of high importance because it keeps the world together and if it is cracked, the world will perish. You see, it balances good and evil so that they would be equal and keep this world running. Righteousness itself will make this world fall…" the Wise Man responded.

"Why can't good itself rule this world? Why not?" Alexis questioned. "This doesn't make sense!"

"At last, you are too young to understand! Good cannot be by itself!" the Wise Man cried like he was suddenly offended.

"Who are you?" Drake shouted.

The Wise Man's tone changed.

"I…am…The…Haunter's…helper! We humans have joined forces with him! I am the guardian of the Anything Code. It is here! Now go die!" Drake took his glaive and thrust the tip at his body and stabbed him.

Reeve and Alexis looked away in disgust.

The Wise Man started shaking uncontrollably and eventually blew up, leaving back a few pieces of hair.

They stood in silence to replay the whole scene. "Wow! That was pure awesomeness! Great job, Drake!" Jarret cried.

"Did he say some humans have joined his side?" Reeve asked. "I don't know, but maybe?" Ian replied.

"Anyway, the Anything Code should be here physically, I hope!" Ian told them. They started searching around. Ian looked under the mat and his cot.

"Forget about this, it is not here! We will never find it!" Josh kicked a piece of dust on the ground.

"Don't give up!" Ian then turned his attention to the wall. He noticed some carving on one of the ice bricks.

"Let's try this…" Ian pushed on the section of wall and only that brick moved backwards. Then, it fell off the building and onto the artic terrain.

The gap was just big enough to get his head through. Then he saw it: a stone the size of a palm with "Anything" on the top of it. Could that be? "Hey guys! It was behind the igloo the whole time in broad daylight!" Ian exclaimed.

They hurried to the back and stared with disbelief. "I do not think that is it," Josh said. "It has 'Anything' on it, let's just take it," Ian suggested. "Are you sure it is safe and probably not a tracking device?" Reeve asked. "I cannot guarantee it, but we need it, so um, I really don't know," Ian answered.

"Just take it!" Alexis ordered.

And they did...Ian picked it up and threw it up into the air. It was light, but he didn't really know what to do with it.

It was very lubricious with a flat surface on the top and bottom. Only the sides stuck out. What was he going to do with a rock? Ian had no idea, but he was willing to wait and be patient until the answer came.

Ian sat down onto the grass and reached for his duffel bag. It was a while since the crystal that had brought them so much trouble. Their whole trip was worthless because now they were overpowered with the Shadow Clan territory backing The Haunter.

Why did he ever get himself into this?

Ian wished Flix would come soon to bear better news than the world feeding on fruit and eventually get malnourished. Even worse after that, they would be physically weak to defend and fight back.

Ian couldn't believe that, for so long, the world was going back to war after what happened long ago when only metal swords, helmets, breastplates, horses, armor, and spears were used for battling.

But in all conflicts, they need to be dealt with eventually. It would be probably a good idea to resolve the conflict, if possible.

It will come a time when they should and will be dealt with, unless there is a deal, which is pretty depends on both sides. What are they willing to give up or do to prevent killing? All conflicts would need to be dealt with in some way, as long as it can prevent it, Ian thought. Thinking too much hurt his mind.

Then, a horn blew, and Ian knew that the boat was about to depart. They hurried back, and got on time.

The boat was powered by machine, and Ian didn't really trust it. It felt unstable as it sliced through the icy water.

He could see what appeared to be many craters on islands of ice. The boat pushed them aside as it hit them.

Then Ian looked into the distance. He could see what appeared to be a dust storm but of ice. It was all white and Ian couldn't see through the thick atmosphere.

"Oh no, here it comes!" Jarret cried. "Duck your heads, everyone!" Alexis cried. Ian did and everybody else followed.

He turned his back against the sky and cuddled-up like a turtle and conserved heat in his body so he wouldn't be cold.

Oh, please, let it be over soon, Ian thought. It went by really fast, somehow, maybe a minute or two, and it was over. Ian peered up and saw that the sky was clear.

"It is safe now!" Ian said.

"Oh, finally!" Drake reacted. "Is it over?" Alexis asked him.

"Of course," Reeve responded. "Don't be so afraid, you!"

"I am not! I was just checking!" Alexis fired back. "Fine, fine, I heard you, please stop yelling at me!" Reeve answered. "En...ough!" Lorry broke in. "That is enough! I cannot be around kids who always fight! If you keep on doing that, I am out, and I will not be with you guys anymore!"

"Sorry," Reeve and Alexis both replied.

"Good, thank you!"

Ian had nothing to do but just wait. At last, the boat docked, and they took the bus back to Tapwa to report their finding. The National Caregiver was the only one there to greet them. The President was absent, so was the Joint Chief of Staff also.

Chapter Ten: The Elite Team

"Welcome back! I have some important new updates. I am sending you guys on a mission! Come. This has to be secretive." Sammy Sam motioned for them to follow him. They walked around the building to the backyard. He looked around to make sure nobody was watching and quickly opened a hatch hidden in the grass but still visible. The metal was well rusted. Ian hopped down, so as the others.

Sammy Sam came in last and pulled the hatch back down. At the same time, with the other hand, he flicked on a light switch. The light took a few seconds to illuminate. Then, he went straight to a book shelf and took out a piece of parchment paper that was rolled-up and tied with a red ribbon.

"This is top secret, you must not tell anybody about this, not even the President," the National Caregiver said. "Why? I thought..." Alexis started. "Follow my words, they are genuine and crucial, please," Sammy told her. "I don't get it, this is not what you are supposed to be doing. You can't give somebody a mission without approval from other officials. I learned this in my Government and Their Responsibilities class from last year!" Alexis hammered back.

"I know, I know, but can you at least trust me?" Sammy asked. Alexis crossed her arms in disapproval as she looked like she was about to speak.

Alexis widened and opened her mouth. Ian stopped her there by saying, "It is fine, keep going, Sammy."

Alexis shifted the focus of her eyes to Ian. It was hard to look back because they were so intimidating.

She looked as if she just got betrayed.

"Ok, all right, let us surely move on…" the National Caregiver assured. He unraveled the wrinkled parchment paper and took four stones from a little basket to put on every corner so it will stay put.

The Crystal-Recovered Squad gathered around circular table. Ian stood directly across from the National Caregiver. Sammy got a bottle of ink and a quill from a cabinet and set it onto the table in front of him. "Here's the thing." He dipped the quill into the bottle of ink and gently tapped it against the side to prevent too much ink.

Then, he drew out what appeared to be a continent. The walls of the room were none other than dry hard dirt.

"You ever know why they call the area here the Forbidden Landscape in school? Well, it is an area where nuclear energy and radiation encompasses. They actually use the term "Forbidden Landscape" so they wouldn't have to use the real word. No men who enter there comes out alive, people say. I am not sure if that is actually true, you know. But all I know is that there is a mysterious green gas that lurks around," Sammy said.

"You want use to go in there? No way. Not at all! Never! Are you crazy? Of course not! You've got to be kidding me!" Reeve exclaimed. "Wait! You've not heard all of it yet! Wait till I finish."

"There is word from a spy whose name he does not want exposed that The Haunter is advancing outside of his territory through that massive wasteland out there…" Sammy trailed off. "Ugh," Jarret exclaimed with repulse. "That place again? Nasty!"

"Yes. Also, he is moving towards Regal Canyon, and I want you guys to stop him. But you will not be alone together. I have several adolescents who will be escorting you and helping you fight too," Sammy explained. "Let's get back up…"

A ladder extended out and one-by-one they climbed out. Lorry got out last. Drake got out second-to-last. Josh was first. Ian was third. Sammy was fourth.

The National Caregiver brought them through a backdoor and into a rather oval-shaped room.

4 people stood near the window on the other side. "Let me introduce them to you guys," Sammy said.

Starting from the left, he said, "This is Aubrey, who is 21." He smiled. "This is Rosalyn, who is 23." She waved. "This is Jocelyn, who is also 23." She was very tall. "And finally, this is Miriam, who is 16." Ian was amazed. Just 16 and already participating in secret missions? Was that even legal? He assumed it was. Besides, he himself was only 13-ish.

"They signed up for this, and volunteered," Sammy said.

"Oh wow," Drake broke in. "By the way, did you notice that Rosalyn and Jocelyn look like identical twins even though they are actually fraternal?" Sammy asked.

"Oh yeah!" Reeve cried. "Good. So, get to know each other, the mission will be in 2 hours," and with that, he left.

After the National Caregiver exited, Drake walked up like a mature man and took out his hand to Aubrey. "So, how do you do?" Drake spoke in such a manner as though he knew him very well. Aubrey shook his hand.

"Nice to meet you, I see that we will be working together from now on…secretly!" Aubrey returned. "You know it is actually permanent, right? So, whatever mission you people are on, we have to tag along…"

"How did you even know about all this?" Drake asked. "Well, I am a freshman in Tapwa City University, the best in the continent, when I stumbled upon an invitation paper on the floor. Well, most people would just think of it as trash because it was on the floor, but I had this notion that made me pick it up. There was a phone number at the bottom. I wasn't sure what it was and I just called. So, I had this long conversation and BOOM! Here I am now!" Aubrey concluded. "What about you guys?"

"Well, actually, it is a long story…" Alexis smiled. "Too long to share, and it cannot be abridged."

"Oh well, I respect your decision and feeling, so, it is fine, really!" Aubrey announced like it was nothing.

"I kinda starting to like this guy!" Jarret spoke into Ian's ear.

"I mean, I don't want to hurt you or anything, but I really can't tell you anything!" Alexis clarified. Aubrey nodded. "I totally understand, don't judge too much about it, you're a good girl."

"Oh my gosh!" Alexis cried.

That scared Ian.

"What? What? What?"

"Can I have your number?" Alexis asked Aubrey like they were in an investigation room. Aubrey looked as if he was shocked too and didn't know how to respond.

"I have never ever in my entire life heard somebody call me a "good girl", you are just incredible!" Alexis exclaimed. "Oh, thank you so much, but uh," Aubrey seemed lost.

Alexis stepped toward Aubrey.

They started engaging in deep conversation.

So the rest of them started talking one after another for the next rest of the time. They broke into small groups. Ian felt a sense of jealousy that Aubrey had the attention of Alexis.

He wanted that for a long time, but he never got it while this guy got it right away…max 5 minutes.

Miriam was kinda cute, according to Ian. He liked her and immediately had a crush on her. Ian tried to talk to her, but it was harder than talking to both Rosalyn and Jocelyn. How in the world did Alexis do so well at being so flirtatious? "What is the matter?" Jarret asked. "Nothing," Ian plainly lied.

Everybody became good friends with each other, but they didn't really know what was waiting for them. Ian learned that Aubrey knew that other 3 girls from other friends.

The door bang open, and two guards were there. "Suit up!"

Aubrey was handed a weapon and a belt of packets of bullets. All in all, he got 50 rounds strapped to his chest.

Rosalyn and Jocelyn both got a mini handgun.

And Miriam, she got a bow and arrows. Ian, Drake, Alexis, and Josh passed on the needing a weapon part while Jarret got a stun-gun somehow, which was really weird.

When they asked Lorry, she said she didn't need any because she is a double black belt in taekwondo.

"Mom, really? I never knew!" Ian exclaimed. "Son, you never pay attention," Lorry responded.

At last, after Miriam tried a few test shots with the bow, one of the guards said, "We are leaving!"

They were led out into a courtyard where a mini helicopter was waiting. There was a pilot, a co-pilot, and just enough seats for each of them. Ian chose to sit next to Miriam, he liked being close to her.

The helicopter ascended.

Chapter Eleven: The Surprise Assault

"Hey Ian, have you done anything like this before?" Miriam suddenly asked. Ian thought about it and nodded. "Yeah, many times. It is pretty amazing for my age. But I just do it for the sake of the world."

"I decided to come because I wanted to fight for my home, my continent, the world. Is all this thing about The Haunter really true?" Miriam questioned. "Oh…yeah. It is sadly true. And you've seen it all, right? You see it all the time on the news. Cities crumbling, unexpected attacks, threats, everything!" Ian replied.

"But you did the right thing for coming," Ian assured her. "Yeah, I dreamed since I was a little girl that I would one day stand up for my planet in an active combat mission."

"I just never did it before, so I'm a little bit nervous," Miriam answered. "I feel for you," Ian responded. "But here this, stay on my side, you'll be fine, I will protect you," Ian slipped out of his mouth. Miriam agreed. "Thanks." They didn't talk for the rest of the way. At last, in midday, Ian peered out of the window and he saw a rather vast canyon. The helicopter slowly descended. Ian knew the time had come.

It went towards a cliff and landed. The two guards and pilots gave out commandments and they filed out.

"Wait, you are not coming with us?" Drake pointed to the guards.

"I follow orders from the National Caregiver, I'm sorry, I cannot stay to help, and I wish I could…"

The helicopter ascended and Ian waved to say goodbye for now. It became smaller and farther away until it totally disappeared from the horizon.

"Let's go down there," Drake pointed. "Into the canyon." It was awkwardly silent. A running river divided two pathways, as they walked through the canyon. "So, what should we do now? In what direction are they coming? Should we wait for them?" Rosalyn asked. "I don't know," Ian admitted. "Let's move towards the sun that should get us started there!" Miriam recommended. Fearful somebody would not agree, Ian blurted, "Yeah! That sounds good! Let's go with that!" "I guess so," Josh replied. "Can you actually believe that nature once carved out this canyon millions of years ago at least?" Josh exclaimed. "Very unbelievable, you're right," Ian answered.

"Wait a minute, we didn't get any instructions at all! They didn't even tell us where The Haunter is. Oh, we were big fat idiots!" Lorry suddenly cried.

"Huh?" Ian was perplexed.

"You never have somebody trap you in a desolated place without any water or food! You never go on a mission without any information about what is going to happen! You never do anything dangerous without instructions! How do you know that the helicopter will come back to take us? What if it doesn't?" Lorry was on a rampage.

"That is impossible," Alexis responded with a rather quivering voice. "That can't be!" Drake reacted. "From a government official? No way!" Ian shouted.

"I think she is right, unfortunately," Miriam said in an innocent manner. Aubrey looked around and then nodded his head.

"In circumstances like these, I fear we just walked blindly right into a trap. Besides, something smells fishy here," Jocelyn pointed out. "Oh, who cares?" Ian said.

They continued to walk.

There was nobody around.

And then, they were forced to stop because there was a fence that read: No Trespassing beyond This Point. The fence ran from one side of the canyon to the other side. The bottom half of it in the middle was submerged in the running river. There wasn't enough room to scoot under the fence, and it was like 15 feet high.

"Well, I think we went the wrong direction," Miriam pointed out. "You really believe that?" Ian asked.

Then, a piece of a rock fell onto Ian's head, hitting him. He reached down and scooped up the stone. It was only the size of a fraction of his palm. Ian looked up and knew it had come from the very top. But from what he had learned the pass year from physics, was that something must have caused it to fall.

The wind possibly. Ian suddenly saw a man's face from the very top, very awkward. Something was wrong.

"Duck! Take cover! Hide!" Ian yelled so loud that it might as well be a scream. The twins were startled, even Lorry.

Jarret darted to the side of the canyon where there was shade.

Drake looked up.

Ian heard something. It seemed like an arrow whistling through the wind. The sound got louder and louder with a shrill and sharp noise. Ian looked around.

It stopped, hitting something that was not very hard or soft.

Ian turned around.

An arrow was sticking out of the left breast of Miriam, where the heart was. She was taking slow and deep breaths. Two seconds later, she fainted and fell to the ground.

Ian caught her before she hit the ground. Her eyes were still open, her mouth also slightly open. Ian put her on his knees. He could feel the strength draining from Miriam.

"No! This will not be!" Ian shouted.

Miriam appeared to smile a tad and then her eyes shut forever.

Ian felt like he lost control of everything. No, this did not happen. Ian was downcast. He didn't know how to act. That was when anxiety kicked in.

Ian was expressionless, but not for long. He didn't act, he just sat there in hero position. This was too sad.

He didn't care what was happening around him. He didn't care about his life. He didn't care about anything.

His emotions fell apart and mixed together.

Drop after drop of tears fell directly onto Miriam's clothes.

Ian had only knew her for like half-the-day and she was already gone. How fast life goes. How short life is.

It was all too terrible.

Ian knew her as a good friend. He wanted to keep the friendship between them after everything was over, but that "Want" could never be achieved now. There would never be another "Miriam" in his life.

"Ian! We have to move! Or we will die!" It sounded like the voice of Joe. Were the dead spirits talking to him?

Was he really dead? Is that why he could listen to the voice of the dead? Ian didn't care, nevertheless.

But he knew that he had to get out of the situation first.

The Haunter was trying to kill them!

Ian lifted Miriam's body onto his arms and planned to carry her.

"Cover me!" Ian cried tearfully and furiously.

Arrows and bullets rained on them.

"No matter what, keep moving so you won't be targeted easily!" Lorry yelled. Josh took his guns and fired up. Drake blocked the bullets from hitting him with the flat surfaces of his glaive. Alexis put her hand into the sky and summoned flocks of birds to attack the attackers, whoever they were.

That method worked.

The eagles clawed and grabbed at them, causing distractions. Some eagles were shot down by rifles, some flew around and bit their skin. Humans were behind all this, Ian realized.

Some have gone to The Haunter's side, but the question is: why?

Reeve kept her bow in her hand, but didn't fire any arrows.

They found themselves running back the way they came from. Aubrey assisted Ian and became his body guard, physically covering him from harm while shooting back.

Rosalyn, Jocelyn, Jarret, Lorry, and Reeve didn't even care to fight. They just ran. Ian did too. He wanted to get out of the situation as fast as possible and most importantly, alive. Alexis made more eagles appear in the sky to attack. They fought in angry hordes like in an army...viciously. Aubrey and Josh were really the only ones fighting for real. Drake just blocked several bullets coming at him.

Then, Ian glanced quickly upwards. He saw that many human faces were visible and they were each carrying fist-sized rocks. They threw them downwards.

"Beware!" Ian cried.

Josh quit fighting and started sprinting. Aubrey shot the rocks out of the air. A rock hit Ian in the right side of his face.

Normally, a person would be knocked out, but Ian felt super powerful because he was determined to get away.

Rocks, arrows, and bullets rained on them. Most missed.

"Jump into the river!" Ian shouted.

Nobody rebelled.

They hopped into the river and the running water took them double their speed before. Ian made sure the body of Miriam did not get wet as he dodged wet rocks.

Ian was always afraid of what was in water. But in this case, nothing else seemed to matter but losing his life.

When he heard stories of other people in a war zone, he was usually extremely fascinated and interested in it. But here, it was the exact opposite, and he liked to keep it that way.

No matter how hard they'd tried, The Haunter had the advantage because they were high up and had a better view.

This was a planned trap. Sammy Sam was a traitor. He had lied.

Bullets plunged into the water, creating little splashes.

A waterfall was ahead. Oh no, we are dead, Ian thought.

"What should we do?" Ian cried. "Pray that it is a low one and that there wouldn't be any rocks underneath when we fall," Lorry said fearfully. "It was nice knowing y'all."

"I'm sorry Ian for every time I yelled at you," his mother said. Ian nodded. "I forgive you," Ian answered.

"I'm scared," Jarret said as he hugged Ian. "Trust me, we will get through this alive, all of us!" he replied.

Ian heard Drake take a deep breath, he didn't know how the others felt. The waterfall was only 20 feet away now.

"Oh no, brace yourself now!!!" Ian cried.

Ian didn't remember the plunge. But it was a fairly low waterfall, about 30 feet. Could somebody survive that?

They all did.

They were at the edge of the canyon, where it ended. Ian woke up while floating in the water. He was all wet.

Ian risked his head by looking up and he saw that everyone was at least 2 feet around him. They had all fainted from over-exaggeration. Also, too much water pressure.

Ian heard the sound of a helicopter. He stumbled onto land, dragging himself out of the water and then belly flopping. He waved his hands in the air to catch the attention of it.

Finally, help had arrived.

But it was no medic or military helicopter.

It was equipped with anti-aircraft machine guns. It touched down and skidded through the water with a thing at the bottom that looked like a skiing cleat.

"We are to take you to Dop now, the epicenter of the Terrorism organization. Come aboard! If you refuse, we will simply shoot you! We are certainly not afraid too. The Haunter is scheduled to meet you tomorrow in Dop…" a terrorist said.

They wore bandanas around their heads, very lousy shirts, and ripped jeans and khakis, with ferocious expressions.

"Leave the dead one here!" the person demanded. "The dead are not allowed because they have already served justice…" "But she did not deserve such justice!" Ian cried, attempting to run at him and punch his face. But his act was stopped when both Josh and Drake pulled him back. "Why, guys? I need to avenge her!" "It is not the time, don't try," Drake said.

Ian dropped the lifeless body into the pond and put his hands up, not waiting for anyone else to do it. "We surrender."

Chapter Twelve: The Death Course

With their wrists bounded in duct tape, they walked single-file into the helicopter like they were at a prison camp. They were like walking into a vehicle to be transported elsewhere like barn animals on their way to a slaughterhouse away from the farm.

They each were given assigned 'seats' (sections of the floor) and sat against the side, each inches away from each other.

The terrorists sat on the other side, each having their own man and staring them in the face, making sure there was no movement. They seemed extremely prideful, like they were proud to have captured The Haunter's most wanted.

The helicopter moved and left the area quickly. It was hard to not blink and stare back at the terrorist's face. His face was dirty and weather-beaten. His clothes were the same. He had a long beard too.

The guy looked like he was some farmer that worked nonstop for the whole day! Did they ever take showers or even brush? I mean, their teeth were pitch yellow.

But Ian didn't care.

It didn't matter to him. What did matter was to get out of the situation fast enough so they can stop this whole baloney.

He probably thought too hard.

He felt his mind wander off and think elsewhere. Ian dared not think of what happened hours ago.

It was way too painful and hurtful.

How could they do that? Were the humans involved really humans? They must have gotten brain-washed.

"Thinking, right?" the guy across from him pointed out like he was some mind-reader. Ian slightly nodded. "Yeah, so?" He wanted to ignore him but yet was afraid of the outcome if he did…so something in the middle should be ok, and indeed it was!

"I am sorry about all this, but we want you all on our team! The truth is, we are not that bad. You know, The Haunter has seen outstanding and tremendous talents you people have! Why, we have been thwarted so much because of you! So, don't think that we are evil and are going to kill everybody and stuff."

"Bottom line, we are not going to harm anybody, just making the world a better place to live. Here, my name is Charles Barry, nice to meet you."

The terrorist extended his hand. Ian was hesitant. Charles forgot that he couldn't move his hands, but soon realized. Charles took out a pocket knife from a strap around his waist that also carried loads of ammunition.

"Let me see your hands!" Charles ordered. Ian obeyed and scooted around so his back was facing him. Oh, please, don't let him cut my skin, Ian thought. Ian gritted his teeth and shut his eyes in terror. In one swift move, Charles unbounded Ian's hands.

"I trust you won't try to escape so high in the air, besides, I believe you are afraid of heights, eh? I saw you scream when you fell down that waterfall…it wasn't really high up," Charles exclaimed.

"Yeah," Ian replied quickly.

"Cheer up, bro! Don't be sad!" Charles urged him. Ian felt like this was weird; he and an unknown and full-grown dirty adult having a conversation that will lasts for whoever knows!" Ian just hated this.

Ian shifted his sight and focus to the people he really knew. They were all different. Nobody was speaking or making any noises. They all seemed tired with heads drooping like they were falling asleep.

Ian felt different. They didn't have the talkative, annoying, and attention-seeking attitude as usual. The atmosphere was rather lugubrious and lacking any excitement.

Of course! Was Ian out of his mind? They had first been fooled, then attacked, and now captured. It made perfect sense, so why did Ian still feel different?

Hours passed and went by.

Half of the Crystal-Recovered Squad had fallen asleep. They deserved it after a long time. Ian could see the sunset and the orange light creeping out on the clouds.

Ian, later, fell asleep too naturally. It was midnight when the helicopter stopped moving. Lights flick on.

"Out! Out! Come on! Rise and shine!" Charles cried. They all woke up at once. Jarret seemed resilient, but Ian snatched him up because he was afraid that he would frustrate the terrorists and receive grave consequences.

Reeve seemed extremely cranky but didn't dare protest as usual.

Everything has changed.

Aubrey, Rosalyn, Jocelyn, Drake, Reeve, and Josh had gotten their weapons stripped off their bodies. Lorry was very distressed, and seemed panicky.

The weapons were put into a basket and taken away.

"Hey! What about this?" Charles pointed at Ian's Wrist Striker. "What is that anyway?" he asked.

"Oh, it is just some toy that I super-glued to my arm," Ian lied flatly. Charles knew it, but let him go with it. "You know what? We will both see soon enough if you are correct, and with that, he ordered, "Take them to the cargo ships! Put them each in a different compartment! Welcome to Dop, Ian Lanterncup!"

Ian received a pang of anxiety. He walked out for the first time and saw that Dop was a floating city made artificially on water.

Cargo ships were everywhere carrying gigantic rectangular boxes.

There was no metropolitan or urban area. Ian wondered if the cargo ships were the city of Dop by themselves.

"Come with me," a big man ordered.

"Each one of you will receive solitary confinement for 24 hours, and after that, you will meet The Haunter."

"Sounds good," Ian blurted.

"By the way, your cells are actually the rectangular boxes you see. Each one of you will get one."

One-by-one they were escorted into their own box. There was a lot of room inside but no light after the door was shut. Ian thought this was surely the end.

When Alexis was signaled to walk into her own stingy space, she looked like she was about to cry. Ian comforted her by patting her back and saying that, "It is okay!"

Ian didn't think it really helped as he watched the garage-like door slid down and Alexis was gone and appeared no more.

"Ian, be wise while I am not there," Lorry warned as she trudged into her metal-plated box. "Behave and be good for me...please." Ian pursed his lips and nodded rather unwillingly, downcast. It was over. "You have been a good friend recruiting me to be part of this," Josh shook Ian's hand as he stepped into his.

"I just want to say 'thank you' before we part," Josh told him, and then he turned to Reeve. "I have to leave you now," and he disappeared. Reeve blinked a few times, and she was speechless. Jarret looked suicidal when it was his turn. He started to panic and tugged at Ian's shirt, hugging him and not letting go.

"Cousin! Listen to me! Get in there! I promise everything will be fine!" Ian cried furiously. "How can you make sure? How can you guarantee?" Jarret sobbed.

He was pulled off Ian, dragged along the pavement, and into his little cell. It was sad seeing him in the state of this.

"Well, it was nice knowing you," Aubrey called casually when it was times up for him. Ian could hear a little quivering in his voice, which meant he was kind of nervous.

"I signed up for this job, now I need to fulfill it!" Aubrey turned and left him there. "Thank you so much for being with us," Jocelyn said.

"I will not forget you…never!" as she walked up the ramp to her prison. "Farewell! We will be friends forever no matter what obstacle!" Rosalyn couldn't let her go but did. "Ian, you are my best friends in the world! So, remember me as your best friends too," and Drake left.

"Bye," Rosalyn told Ian. "I pray that whatever lies ahead will be a blessing," and with that, she was gone.

Now it was only Reeve and Ian taken by a big bulgy man.

"Wow! Your friends have so much faith in you! I fear this is your stopping point! No more escaping!"

Ian let out a gulp of air slowly. He sighed. "Maybe you are right!"

Reeve was fidgeting with her eyes darting around like something was going to pop up and suddenly scare them.

It was midnight.

It was the perfect scene for a horror movie…like a monster was going to jump out and freak out the audience.

Ian didn't like the place.

"Little girl, this is your resting place," the guy exclaimed.

Reeve stomped and marched up the rusted ramp like somebody in a funeral procession who is lacking appropriateness.

The door slid and Ian heard a click, which was the sound of it locking. Ian knew time was up for him.

"And finally you, gentleman."

"Your career is over!" the bulgy guy smirked. "This is it for you! Soon, you will be less important than a piece of dust!" he spat. Ian didn't care as he trudged up what seemed like the stairway to heaven, except that it was not heaven but hell.

He paused and looked up at the moon. It was full tonight. Walking in, he turned around to face outside.

The sky was clear and beautiful. He glimpsed it and everything became black, extra pitch black.

Everything was gone.

Ian longed for some light, but there was none. He felt his way toward a wall and sat down, back against it. All was hopeless, he thought. What else could he do? He had escaped so many time from evilness, so what now?

He was determined to keep trying, but was it meant to be over already? He remembered what his dad said when he was about to die. "This is my destiny!" Arnold Lanterncup had spoken softly. So, was this the Crystal-Recovered Squad's destiny? Were they destined to end up like this?

Why couldn't he be like regular teenagers who hung out with each other all the time? He yearned to be one of them at that moment and situation. They didn't need to care about anything, but possibly schoolwork and girls...

But why? Ian thought.

Why did he get himself into this? He had asked for this and dragged along the entire Crystal-Recovered Squad plus a few lone members that had somewhat joined.

What was the meaning of all this?

Now, don't get too emotional! Thinking too much is bad! Doing anything too much is bad! So, why didn't he just settle down and have some fun as a kind of break or free time from the main thing he was doing most?

Ian was completely stressed-out and overwhelmed.

It was all too much and mixed up. He was to let go of some things, but he cared about them too much.

He needed to reduce some responsibilities.

Joe had revealed his will for him to be leader, even over his mother. Lorry had kind of agreed, but wasn't always on track. So Ian was the leader the whole time!

How can it be? The job was too hard. He needed a vacation. He needed to relax. He needed to chill, somehow in this situation.

He needed to do something else and focus and concentrate on other stuff. It could be anything, at least something. Ian needed multiple occupations.

Ian rubbed his forehead with his fingers to reduce stress with his eyes closed. He felt the energy draining away from his nervous system and muscles.

He finally gave way and fell onto his side, falling asleep right there without a blanket or pillow.

Ian didn't want nightmares. He was prone to have them all the time.

He didn't get any.

But his sleeping was disturbed when light flushed in.

"Who's that? Who's there?" Ian cried weakly, lifting his head an inch above the ground. Something definitely non-human was standing there. "Flix? Is that really you?" Ian pushed himself up.

And indeed it was.

Ian was so happy that he tiptoed toward him and hugged him.

Flix was in pretty good condition. He was smiling too.

"What are you doing here?" Ian asked. "What about the others?"

"Shhh, don't talk so loud, they might here you!" Flix urged him. "I am here to get you and everybody!"

Ian was glad. He was gladder than the gladdest. In all universe, Flix was there all the time! He was grateful and thankful for knowing him.

"Thank you so much! You were absent so long that I thought you would never come back! And indeed you did come back! Thank you!" Ian cried, bursting into tears of joy.

"I was at rock bottom before!"

"What time is it, by the way?" Ian asked. "Exactly 4 in the morning. Hurry, we need to get everyone and leave as fast as possible on a boat I set up close by. They will be up by 5…" Flix pointed out.

"All right," Ian replied. Flix went to freeing the rest. "I have the weapons with me. Found them!"

He activated a hand-saw with a sharp blade and edge and sliced through the thick metal. It was as easy as slicing cheese from top to bottom in one quick swipe.

Reeve stood up, shocked, watching Flix and standing immobile. "Hurry! Don't waste time! Time is precious!" Flix delivered. He then freed the others one-by-one. They all had the same reaction. But when it got to Alexis, she sat there dumbfounded, and then slowly stood up and ran to Flix to hug him.

Flix almost lost his balance.

"I knew you'd come back! I knew it!" Alexis cried. "Well, you thought correct, now let's go!" Flix replied.

Together, they got to sea level, and directed by Flix, was brought to a mini boat made of gigantic logs.

"Are you sure? It seems very tight!" Josh asked, pointing at the interior. "You will fit perfectly, believe me..." Flix answered without doubt.

They steadied the boat and made sure everybody got in before moving the paddles. "The waves will carry us," Flix said.

Away they drifted. Ian kept looking back and worrying that somebody would find out and send a rocket at them.

He had a fear of deep sea.

The boat rocked back and forth. Ian was afraid that it would capsize and potentially drown them all.

Land was drifting farther and farther away. The boat continued to glide along the deep blue sea of murky salt water.

"How come I see puffs of air, or possibly vapor bursting out of the water? No way, they couldn't be..." Jocelyn pointed out. "So?" Alexis asked.

"Oh man, I forgot!" Flix suddenly shouted. "What is wrong? What's wrong?" Ian questioned. "I accidentally got ourselves into the lair of the Underwater Volcanoes!"

"What's the matter?" Lorry questioned. "What did you do?" she demanded. "I accidentally put ourselves in the lair of the Underwater Volcanoes," Flix repeated, sounding extremely concerned. "Oh! I am such an idiot," Flix exclaimed.

"There is no way out!"

Ian thought he had the solution. "I got it! What about the bubble thing..." "It is not going to work!" Flix explained.

"Why?" Ian questioned. "It doesn't work so close to the water. You see, there is a battery inside that Wrist Striker, and if it gets too close to the water, it may malfunction and detonate just by sensing H20."

"Trust me! What I do you know is that I have gotten you guys on a death course straight to Vapdello Island. I need to refresh your memory. Remember where you and Drake got your weapons from? Remember that refrigerator-like case that magically appeared in your school? Well, there is a connection between that and both your weapons," Flix yelled over the howling wind. Ian was confused.

Then he saw the island.

It was covered with an enormous volcano spewing ash and lava down its slopes that may soon turn into pyro clast. "It is always active, and never stops exploding, and we are headed towards it…" Flix screamed. "We are going to crash into fire." All around them, clumps of vapor flew up into the sky in various spots of the ocean. The boat suddenly lurched sideways, as though it was hit by a cannonball. Salt water sprang up and into the boat.

It was a big scare for everyone. Alexis put her hand over her chest as if she was calming her heart. Reeve took long deep breaths. Jarret just sat there with his mouth slightly open and eyes solid and very much still.

Ian figured something out. He saw that there was an entire long line of vapor from volcano pressure coming up on either side every few seconds.

He inferred that the boat lurched because they were too close to the line. That meant they were trapped between two lines of vapor that floated upwards every other second. The lines were straight, but then curved all the way to the base of the volcanic activity.

The waves pushed the boat towards the massive volcano of Vapdello Island. They were going to burn to death form the lava flowing down.

The lava flows crashed into the water, turning it into acid. The acid was spreading like a ripple effect. Closer and closer the boat went to it. Lesser and shorter time was left.

"We have to do something fast and act now and immediately!" Aubrey cried. "Everyone understand?" Drake asked.

Everybody nodded.

Flix looked lost. He didn't know what to do, honestly. They were under pressure. It was either life or death, pretty much.

The boat glided through the water, on its one-way to death. This was a straight death course. Ian could see the red-hot lava. He could feel the heat from it already.

The water vapor on either side, appearing by moment, prevented them from escaping the lane they were on.

How in the world did the waves get them trapped, and almost about to be killed by a natural disaster?

Vapdello Island was a mess. It really was. The entire thing was pretty much the volcano itself occupying it.

This couldn't be happening.

Ian thought trouble was gone and distant, but it was only the beginning, he realized, and trouble has caught up with him once again! Oh boy, Ian thought.

"Paddle! Paddle!" Aubrey ordered. Alexis went at it and attempted to divert the boat in a different direction. Reeve didn't do a thing but just stared blankly at the volcano.

"What are you doing? Do something…anything in the whole wide world!" Ian yelled.

"Why do I have to listen to you, huh?" Reeve challenged, arms crossed. "I am about to die, so why can't I enjoy the last moments of my precious life?"

She was clearly shocked and out of her mind. Ian felt bad for her. It made perfect sense, but then he got back to his consciousness and reality.

Everything was rapid-paced.

Ian did some quick calculations. The water vapor caused by underwater steam from the volcanoes below seemed to appear every 5 seconds. But was it consistent? It was risky, but they had to try, and besides, it was the only choice they got.

There were 4 paddles and Alexis, Josh, Drake, and Rosalyn took one each. The rest used their hands, dipped them into the water, and started scooping them backwards for extra force.

Ian made sure that there was equal persons on either side of the boat.

"Come on! Let's go!" Ian cried.

Ian put his own hand into the water and pushed against it. The boat seemed resistant for a moment but finally moved.

Time was running out. The acid was going to reach the boat. They would be dead even before the boat reached the island.

Vapor rose toward the sky simultaneously. "Now!" Ian shouted.

For the next 5 seconds, it was the most painstaking time of Ian's life, and probably everyone else too. They pushed with all their might.

The boat hovered over the line of vapor and crossed at the right timing. Vapor flew up after those tedious 5 secs.

Ian sighed. It was better now.

The boat drifted away from the volcano and the island of Vapdello. He had no idea what it meant and why it was there, but it didn't matter or even cared to him.

"High-fives!" Jocelyn exclaimed. "Are you kidding me? That was the most amazing thing we have done as a team!" Drake pointed out. "Amazing! Simply amazing! Unbelievable! I just cannot believe it!"

Everyone had held their breath but now let loose their air.

The whole thing was extremely stressful, and required a whole lot of energy, but they did it! They conquered it! They beat it! They worked as a team and did it!

It must have been a miracle. How could they have done that?

It must have been a work of the Lord.

Daylight flooded in. It was time for sunrise. They were flooded with warmness, which made them feel a tad better.

The sea shimmered and sparkled.

And they had arrived at Saik, it being just ahead (another city). Ian had enough with the ocean and the sea. He was never going to venture and tag along aboard a cruise ship ever again, even if it was really fun. He needed to be back on land, it was crucial to him.

Bottom line, he had had enough. Really, enough is enough—no arguing with at all. He meant it, and he was serious about it. No more joking around. It was the truth, and he knew it very and really well.

Chapter Thirteen: I.I.T.C.

The boat reached the bay and into a little port. There was an immigration center with dozens of police officers and cops patrolling the area. The boat got to shallow water and hit a rock, then stopped.

There was a huge fence blocking the ocean road from the beach. There was a lot of honking and street traffic. This was city-life. Ian was relieved to be back in a city environment. It felt good.

The roaring noise of motorcycles dominated the atmosphere.

"Can we jump the fence? How are we even going to get past immigration? If they did even let us, they would still be suspicious. Don't you think so too?" Jarret asked.

Ian shrugged. "No choice," he murmured.

It was true.

They waited in a line of people who have also gotten there by means of transportation over the ocean at approximately the same time. The line slowly got shorter as more and more people left. Then, it was their turn.

"Passports?" the officer behind the glass window called.

"Oh, um, uh, we are kind of like…refugees seeking a place to hide," Reeve lied out of the blue. Ian wanted to protest because she hadn't approved it with everyone, but he knew he should rather keep his mouth shut, just wishing for the best.

The sheriff deputy was shaking his head like it wasn't funny. "Liars." "No!" Aubrey quickly cried out. "You got it wrong. This is a misunderstanding!" Jocelyn pointed out to the sheriff deputy.

"I don't believe it."

"But you have to believe us!" Alexis pleaded. "Please!" The cop put on a thinking expression for several seconds before finally let loose.

"You are set to go. You are free. But there is one other way to do it. Follow me, I will have my colleague finish the rest of the people up. But follow me, because that is the only way!" Ian seemed reluctant. Was he really going to trust this guy? He didn't know for sure.

But went with the flow as usual.

They walked into a small building and went pass a door that read: Interrogation and Questioning Room.

Inside was a simple table. One side was for the interrogator, and other for the person being interrogated.

A section of the wall on the door side was a window, where cops outside could take notes. Ian couldn't see how they could a fit, somehow. It was a big headache.

"There is no room!" Jarret protested. "Make some," the guard responded, taking chairs from where they were stacked in the corner. He went to the lock the door too.

"Now, I need to know simple and clear why you lot are here," he explained. "You see, we are in a task force, and wasting time will not help. It is extremely important and top secret, sent by our own government," Drake answered. "I second that," Josh broke in. "I third that!" Ian corroborated.

"Ok, but you have to convince me...why?" he repeated. "We told you! You can check of the list that we are not spies, but please, let us go through already!"

"Fine, if you are in such a hurry, go tell it to the chief. You will no doubt get yourself arrested," he yelled.

Then, several guys entered the room. They were told to get in a line against the wall preparing to leave the room through the door and facing it. They obeyed orders. That was when a bag was flung over Ian's head, containing his body. He fell to the floor, struggling. There was darkness. He could also feel something pointy sinking into his flesh, probably a needle. It was most likely a drug that made one fall asleep for a certain amount of time. It flowed into his muscles ad weakened them. That was the last thing he dared remember. He had fainted by force.

Ian became conscience in broad daylight, which was abnormal. He lifted his head and realized he was on a sidewalk right next to a busy road and highway.

The trees hid the highway.

Ian pushed himself up, his whole body aching and immediately saw a huge building looming over him.

It was semi-sphere shaped and completely comprised of glass.

Flix sat up, dazed. "First time I ever got captured and couldn't shadow-travel," he brought up. "I will find whoever did this to us."

A parking lot was behind him. He spotted the rest of the Crystal-Recovered Squad lying in trances on the same sidewalk, each a half foot from each other.

Was this some kind of experiment done on them to test a chemical or something? Ian hoped not.

He ran to wake everyone else up.

Josh rubbed his eyes, and Drake was rather cranky at him being woken up. Rosalyn got up without hesitation. "What was that?" Drake cried. They slowly gathered their minds and decided to check out the place and area. How come passing pedestrians didn't notify anyone of kids sleeping on the ground. Was it even odd?

"Nice," Alexis said, staring at the design of the building and its architecture. They walked in through a series of double-doors and went down an escalator to underground.

Below, there was a huge digital map occupying a screen. People crowded around to look at it.

"What is this?" Aubrey muttered. A woman that looked like an army commander, decision maker, and general walked passed them and turned around to face them.

"Welcome to the International Invasion Treatment Center! I see, from those nametags, you all were abducted legally and sent here. Well, the officers did the right thing. So welcome!"

Ian looked down at his shirt, and sure enough, there was a paper nametag there that didn't have his name but "Lost and Found." It was on the other people too.

"What does that mean?" Josh asked.

"The officials of Tapwa claim that they lost several important teenagers and adult after they went on a special task mission. Some are not agreeing to that. So, they are currently investigating. But guess what! We found you guys, already, so no more worries!"

"What is this place about?" Alexis asked.

"Well, we control the major conflicts happening around the world. I am Sargent Sarta, nice to meet you!" "I will be your guide," she added. "Tell us about this map," Alexis pointed out. They were in circular room.

Sargent Sarta took a baton from a basket and pointed it at the map. It was a map of the world. "The places in red are already controlled by the enemy, sadly."

That included the entire continent with Terp and Lotan.

"No way, have there been any fighting?" Drake asked. "Not that I know of, really. There have been little skirmishes. But the enemy had reinforcements every single time."

"This is a way to track the enemy."

"The places in blue are still in control by us. The International Invasion Treatment Center is like the Hexagon in Tapwa, you know, also controlling the military.

The place was like a sitting area of a bowling rink, where players often waited for their turn. Off the main corridor and room was a computer lab that supposedly did research. Screens were everywhere and on 24/7. Everyone was busy. Computers where everywhere. Ian wondered how much the electric bill was and who in the world would pay for it.

"Come, let me show you some things…" Sarta urged.

They followed her and entered through two glass doors into a silent computer lab with employees wearing headphones so they wouldn't be disrupted by noises.

Based on their countenances, they were all looking concentrated and ponderous, which made perfect sense.

It was a big area, like a place they tested race cars. The floor was made of concrete. There were about 50 desks, each with a computer on it. A person was sitting at each one.

"How busy does it get here?" Alexis asked. "They work 12 hours shift before group 2 comes in and resumes the job," according to Sarta. "Oh, wow," Aubrey pointed out.

"So, what exactly are they looking up?" Drake asked. "Well, I figure we can't tell you guys. You see, there is a screen-blinder that they put on each one so everybody from a certain angle cannot peek to see what is going on." "That is too bad," Ian replied. "Besides, do you know who abducted us and put us on a sidewalk in front of this building to sunbathe, anyway?" Flix cried. Sargent Sarta slightly nodded. "Yeah…part of our "impostors" who carry-out things and speed things up, you know."

"So, they are good guys who do things that aren't so positive, right," Aubrey broke in, assuring himself.

"Kind of, yes," Sarta responded.

An employee had gotten up from her chair and off to a printer where a single piece of paper came out.

She strode toward Sarta and stopped when reaching her. "For you," she said, stamping a "Top Secret" logo on the top-corner just a few moments ago on a clipboard. She eyed them wearily and returned to work.

"Hmm, let's see what we've got here…" Sarta started.

And then, an alarm went off somewhere. The sound was so loud that it made small tears flow to the surface of Ian's eye. Somebody was complaining about their mouse. "The whole system jammed! Is the Wi-Fi working? Is the Internet working? I keep clicking the same button and nothing is happening! This has not happened before!"

Sarta hurried to the employee. Ian ran over too. Things weren't going to turn out well, Ian had a hunch.

147

The screen turned pitch red with an "X" on the center of it. A message popped up reading, "We are watching. We know everything!" in big branded bold letters.

Soon, everyone else was getting the same message as though it was some kind of threat. Sarta was shaking her head as if this was unbelievable.

Then, the computer seemed as if it was operating itself and exiting the tab. It went back to the desktop automatically and opened documents and scrolling down. It took a few seconds because there were about 100 files before at last, it clicked on the very one.

A search bar popped up and started loading and processing something, slowly. The employee was so frustrated that he started tapping "Delete" and "Escape" at the same exact timing. It was no use.

The loading ended and three words popped up: "Information Retrieved, success!" And then, the screen was pitch black.

Gone, like the computer and network was dead. Gone. What really occurred? No one had a clue or knew. The situation was too hard to comprehend.

"What the heck just happened?" Sarta yelled. She tried turning the computer back on but it wasn't coming back to life.

"Face it, we have been hacked," the employee said.

"That is impossible! Our system is protected by cyber-shield after cyber-shield, and built by the most prolific tech geniuses in the world to ensure that the system won't fail!" Sarta protested. "Well, there was a flaw, and now every single piece of information is in the cyber-attackers' hands. They must have a highly intelligent mastermind behind all this, better than ours," the employee retorted expertly.

"We are doomed!" Sarta shouted.

She tried the "On" button again, and miraculously it turned on. Sarta sighed and got to work. She put in her password and everything came back to life.

All the icons and programs were gone. She went to the Internet and typed in a random website name. Sarta clicked on the link and URL and it appeared.

She typed CTRL-SHIFT I and CTRL-SHIFT C both two times. All the old programming was gone and replaced.

"No way! How in the world did this happen? What sort of technology could have done this to us? What would have been capable of such advanced..." Sarta didn't finish, furious. "I told you, we got hacked! It is that simple. How many times do I have to repeat?" the employee retorted once again.

"Shut up!" Sarta cried.

Men in suits and ties barged in through the doors, slamming them against the wall. "What is going on?"

The room broke into chaos.

Everybody was yelling at each other.

"Stop! Stop! Stop!" someone cried, but was ignored and had his voice drowned from the overlapping voices.

He was no match for them.

Ian stood as still as a tree trunk.

Finally, the screaming at each other departed from the situation.

"We simply cannot decide what to do next if we are screaming our heads off!" a man said, the one who led the people with suits and ties into the computer lab.

"I call for an Emergency Mission! I'd say that The Haunter was the one behind all this crap! I have my reasons, but I insist that we all get to work!"

Then, a blinding light caught everyone's attention. It was coming from the projector hanging from the ceiling that had been off first and now on, somehow.

"Who did that? Somebody here must have activated the projector and entered the code. Show yourself, and possibly yourselves!" the man demanded.

"No one could have done that who is not present in this room. None! Nobody!" He started pacing around the room, his eyes locked on every computer screen, one-by-one.

All was quiet.

"Show me your hands!" All the computer people raised their hands from below the desk. "Good."

No one seemed to have done it.

151

Then, a message appeared on the wall in a straight font. Big letters. It read: "Tomorrow morning, Kael will be brought down to their knees!"

"Send the Crystal-Recovered Squad now, and we will put up a fight with them. If you refuse, we will blow-up the city with our missiles. I just want the Crystal-Recovered Squad members, and nothing else. Gather your whole army! You have until 5am to get them to the city to defend it, or else…" a voice spoke out of the projector from above.

"What is the Crystal-Recovered Squad?" somebody asked. There was a long silence. The voice was gone. "It is these few here," Flix finally broke it.

He pointed to Ian and his friends, including his mom.

"What is this? Who are these? Spies?" the man cried.

Sargent Sarta interrupted. "No! These were the ones who have discovered The Haunter first and have led them on a run since." "What?" the man cried.

"This is all a hoax!" the man said. "If that voice spoke the truth, we may as well deliver them there…"

No one spoke. Ian knew his time was up for being silent. "Hey, we will go, for the sake of everyone!"

"Are you sure? You never know what would be waiting for you there," Sarta raised her eyebrows.

"This is what we do. This is our job," Ian answered earnestly.

He was candid and honest with it.

"You don't think it is a lie?" the man asked. "I don't think so, I guess not, I guess so," Ian replied.

"Alright, dismissed. The Crystal-Recovered Squad will leave at midnight. It should take 4 hours and 30 minutes to land safely and early at Kael. This is a challenge for us. They are challenging us to a battle!" Sarta announced. "It would be the right choice and presumably wise to engage."

"Agreed?"

Everyone nodded. The man walked over to
Sargent Sarta and spoke a few words into her ear.
Ian couldn't decipher, but saw that she was
nodding, which might as well have been a good
thing, or maybe not. "I will go call the Cove to
organize an army to take-on The Haunter. Let us
go! I don't even know if it is him intending all this.
I mean, it must be," the man waved before
stepping out.

Chapter Fourteen: The Protest

Ian thought that this was sudden death for him and his friends. Heading straight into a battle zone wasn't the best idea. What kind of a leader was he? Ian felt that he was doing the right thing, possibly, at least. But there was still a lingering of fear as though this was wrong.

Midnight arrived really fast. They were sitting in the main lobby, just above the two-way escalators on comfy modern coaches.

Sargent Sarta appeared at the top of the escalator lane that went up. She walked over to the overview and leaned on it, observing the crowds below.

"It is time," she announced.

They went outside. Ian was surprised at how chilly the air had become because it was late into September already.

I.I.T.C. was the size of an airport. It was a big place, in other words. They walked for a half mile before stumbling upon a Jeep. "This is our ride?" Josh asked. "Yeah, we are carpooling, and then boarding a ship to move through the ocean all the way to Kael."

"Nice," Josh answered.

Jocelyn got into the Jeep first, followed by everybody else.

Sarta was their driver. "Wait, you are coming with us?" Drake asked. "Yeah, of course! I want to look after you all," she replied. "Oh, thanks," Alexis told her. "You are always welcome," Sarta said.

Ian always loved road trips because they were allowed him to be lazy. But what he didn't like was having motion sickness.

"The world has changed," Sarta brought up, out of the blue.

Nobody said a word.

Finally, the silence barrier was broken by Sarta. "When we all heard about this, we were all shocked. By "we" I mean those back at IITC. We couldn't comprehend the situation. It wasn't like anything before that was in written records."

Then, something hit Ian. He remembered his mom telling him something about his ancestor. What was his name again? Oh yeah, it was Clive, who apparently had met The Haunter before. The Haunter was somehow some spirit that dove into the Earth; it didn't make sense. "Tell me about your story," Sarta asked.

For the remainder of the road trip, the members of the Crystal-Recovered Squad took their turns to speak, adding in details. The story was long…all the way from the start to where they were now. Sarta didn't interrupt even once. She payed attention and listened attentively.

They finished.

"You know, my dad was once part of the navy. He was angry when he heard of the entire continent of Lotan and Terp being taken over by non-human creatures. He asked himself, "How could it be?" as he expressed his concern. There has never been so much trouble. This was like the old times, where nations fought for territories and conquering land from other ones. This is not how the modern world works, except now it is worse. The High Government should have dealt with the Forbidden Landscape before it was too late. Everyone knew something was going on in there, something terrible. And then there was that city known as Zark. Our politicians have become weak and failed to take control of the issues. Now, we even have that famine! Even so, our oil drilling and mining industry has been taken by force. We have managed to salvage some of the equipment so we could drill elsewhere," Sarta spoke. She was indeed deeply distraught.

"I understand," Lorry put her hand on Sarta's shoulder. She was sitting in the passenger side of the front seat.

"Evermore, there has been some suspicious activity going on within IITC and the High Government. It is probably corruption. There are some traitors undercover. They are feeding information to the enemy. I am not sure why they would do that! They are being used, and probably motivated by bribery and cash from it. Money in their pockets. This is always and has been a human desire for eternity," Sarta continued.

Ian thought of everything she had said, about the famine, and other. He remembered the crystal and retrieved it from his bag. It was a miracle to not have lost it in all the chaos. Everybody's eyes went to its glamorous glow, reflecting off the surfaces of the Jeep. It was a light purple.

"Oh yeah! That…" Sarta grinned through the mirror. "I remember the period where the news was talking about you mysterious people. We thought the threats were from you guys. But things have changed. And know, it is all about some Haunter spirit that wants to kill us!"

"Yes, that is right!" Aubrey pointed out.

Ian really didn't know what the crystal was for. All this time, he had been hoisting it around and risking his life for it. The "Crystal of Len" could have been taken easily by the terrorists who side with The Haunter, and many other evil-doers, villains, and criminals.

But how was it safely nestled and also nested in that duffel bag for so long? His duffel bag was the remaining one. His friends' were all lost and not carried in their hands anymore. Ian still had his. It held the unknown Anything Code that didn't make sense.

Maybe the crystal didn't matter to The Haunter anymore even though it was very visually-appealing and probably was worth billions of dollars.

He stared at the crystal. It seemed as if it was dormant and forever would be. There was not the slightest hint of movement inside it. Ian didn't understand the mysteries of it. What was the material inside? Why was it so special? Anyway, Shadow Clan hadn't been annoying him lately, so he wouldn't have to worry about giving it away or possibly ripped apart from refusing. "It looks nice," Alexis touched its surface.

Its glossy feature and slippery texture gave it a cryptic appearance.

It was also very lustrous and shiny, giving off much light.

Ian wished that one day he would understand the crystal fully. It felt like the end was far away.

An hour and a half later, they reached a mini airport. They went through the scanners and got on board a private jet. It had soft and nice cushions inside.

Ian watched out of the window as the world got smaller and smaller, which made him feel like a giant.

A pretty flight attendant strode by and served orange and apple juice, as well as bags of nut, especially cashews. And then, a cup of fruit because there was nothing else.

There was nothing to do but wait.

Finally, the plane reached and touched the ground, which made Ian lurch back instantly. It came to a halt, and his team were escorted down the steps and through a tunnel.

First thing Ian noticed was, the airport was empty of people.

Something was wrong. This was weird.

"What is going…?" Josh started. "There is a mass evacuation on right now. The mayor has declared a city of emergency. If it wasn't for monitoring y'all and believing you teenagers and adult, we wouldn't have brought you straight into somewhere that is going to be attacked and invaded, especially if you never had experience in the military.

"Totally," Reeve rolled her eyes.

"Also, no cars or motorcycles or trucks are allowed on local roads right now. So, we have to walk. The city is a couple miles from here. I am sure you can see some of the skyscrapers…" Sarta told them. "I have been here before."

They got out of the terminal and gate and proceeded towards the highway. Indeed, there was a massive evacuation. It was a jammed highway. Cars just sat there, waiting for the line to move, and cars to leave through exits.

"Oh man, this is severe," Jarret stated.

"We are north of Kael, c'mon," Sarta urged.

After a few moments, Ian realized not everyone was evacuating, and it was towards the center of the city when he saw why.

The people were out of their minds.

They were marching in big hordes through the streets and on the sidewalks, yelling. Some had picket signs held into the air that read: The government is not honest! They will not say anything or tell us a thing! We demand them to reveal the truth!

Policemen were lined up at every intersection not letting people through. Some clashed with the cops. The officers defended with their glass shields and hitting back with their bats. It was still early morning.

Cans were thrown into the air after being lighted and threw off sparks of fireworks. They ignited and combusted.

Some of the city-residents charged and barged through the line of deputies. He crashed into one and threw him into a half-brick and half-stone wall. One was thrown into a steel sign. And yet another one, onto a gravel pavement.

An officer grabbed him by his hips and shook him.

Another got him in a headlock and they slowly dragged him away. Others grabbed his wailing arms and legs as his chest puffed up and down. A citizen tackled an officer (a female one) and he was tackled by his colleagues whose places where replaced by reinforcements.

So much violence!

"How are we supposed to pass by all this?" Alexis questioned. "We will have to take the long way through the sides and alleyways, and of course, the ballpark and stadium.

"No matter what, follow me!" Sarta announced.

They fast-walked all the way to a cliff through a bridge. "Here is the ocean, we suspect that they will be coming this way!" Sarta assured. Stairs were carved into the stone that lead down below all the way to a beach with yellow sand. The tides were great today, probably because it was full moon tonight.

A huge sandbag wall was put up with holes in between so you could fire through them. "When was this put up?" Ian asked Sarta. "Just yesterday, it was the best we could do with such a poor city like Kael. But if it was Tarso, it'd be much fine. And even better, Moor.

"All right, I get the point! Back to the presence, please!" Ian snapped. Sarta froze. "Don't rush me ever again!" Ian understood his mistake. "Sorry," he hung his head.

Then, there was the sound of a horn.

Chapter Fifteen: The Battle of Kael

Ian turned around and saw that the troops have arrived. From above, a fighter jet appeared under the clouds. It was spiraling forwards, disappearing into the clouds and appearing again over and over.

"It is a drone, a F15, the standard version," Sarta explained. "How did they get their hands on that? They must have access to our military," she added. It was coming from across the ocean. Ian turned his attention back to the sea.

Zartees were dropping and skydiving from the sky. Thousands. Their parachutes blasted out above them as they fell slowly into the cold dark blue water below.

They trudged slowly towards the beach.

Troops surrounded Ian and his friends, plus his mom. Someone was giving commands. They divided into groups.

Then, shots were fired.

A missile went straight down at a steep slope and ignited a tank. It burst into flames, and slowly crumpled away, combusted.

Ian hoped no humans were inside.

He took his place behind the sand-bag wall with all of his friends huddled together and around each other. Kael was a city on an island with an oval river around it.

It was amazing how fast the Zartees got up the small mountain.

They went at the sand-bag wall. It was four rows high. Jarret had the best idea of lifting a heavy one and launching it at one of the Zartees. It didn't even get close.

"Down Jarret! Leave it to me!" Ian cried.

But before he could, a Zartee jumped over the wall and crashed into Ian, grabbing him. Ian shrieked.

He let go, and Ian scrambled away, crawling. The Zartee lunged at him but it was cut short with Drake creating a nasty gash and cut in his back and an arrow flying into the back of his calf.

"Thanks, guys," Ian commented.

"Always there," Reeve smiled. "Will be there when you need it the most, bro," Drake answered and replied.

It was great having companions.

And then, he saw *her.* Lady Harsh. She looked worse than ever. "I am back!" she yelled, her voice ascending.

"Run, head back to the city!" Sarta ordered.

Lorry was eyeing Lady Harsh viciously.

Then, they sprinted, leaving the commotion, and turning their backs against it. Sarta took lead. Ian was sure not to run in a straight line, for he would have a greater chance of getting sliced by one of those ninja stars of hers.

His muscles were panicking and hurting. Ian really wanted to stop running. His lactic acid wasn't enough.

There was a wince, and a body flopped onto the ground. It was struggling. Ian turned and saw Sargent Sarta lying there, breathless and whimpering in agony.

"Get up! We have to hurry!" It slipped out of his mouth. Sarta wasn't moving anymore as he watched dumbfounded.

"Guess she lacked the skills to survive!" a repulsive voice said. Ian knew it was Lady Harsh. He had stopped dead in his tracks. Ian disregarded the danger and faced her. "What do you want?" he shouted.

"I wasn't asking for anything," Lady Harsh or BB responded, throwing a ninja star up and down and repeat. Her stars seemed to always just pop out of the openings of her long-sleeved shirt. "Just having some fun, you know," she grinned, an evil one.

In a split-second, Ian raced the opposite way. He knew yelling at Lady Harsh was a waste of time and didn't help him.

They had lost Sarta, already. She was a general or something. That fast? Ian couldn't believe it. He didn't feel any emotion. Everything felt bland.

She had expressed what she was thinking to them all along, and now he was going to publicize her thoughts.

They made it across the bridge and a few blocks before running into a department building, store, or probably a factory. Or maybe a multi-functional one.

He'd seen Sloogpaps and Dark Elves roaming the area. How did they get here without fighting through the frontline? Could there have been hidden passages underneath the city to connect to other places? There must be a hidden network of them.

In other terms, the invasion was planned.

Ian could hear an exchanging of fire and a shootout going on.

"Here! Hide here!" Alexis demanded.

They hurried in and entered, shutting the door. "We should be safe here," Josh exclaimed, like it was too hopeful to be true.

Someone was running down the corridor. Ian found a lock on the door and turned it. He turned off a light that was on before so that it appeared dark other than the sunshine. He draped an attached curtain to the window on the door. Whoever it was might pass, thinking nobody was inside. "Get behind the door, in case," Ian told everyone, and they obeyed.

Somebody tried the door, shaking the knob. Then, complete silence. Ian heard something break moments later and clatter on the floor. It was none other than the lock.

Ian felt his heartbeat stop for a millisecond. The door creeped open. Ian knew he had to act no matter what.

With a roar of some kind, he balled his right hand and punched whoever it was square in the jaw, injuring him.

The impact sent a cry of pain and anguish. It sounded like the leader of the Zartees. He recognized the voice.

Zhowltagook? No way!

Without thinking, Ian kicked him in the space between his eyes. Zhowltagook's hair flew back.

The Crystal-Recovered Squad fled out the room and ran through hallways. They found another room and went into it. It was composed of a bed and a desk with a lamp on it. A bunk bed was also visible too.

It resembled a dormitory.

"Quickly! Behind the bed! He is searching for us!" Ian cried.

Drake went under the desk where there was empty and open space in the middle of it. He pulled the chair in to hide himself. "Fine, you stay there," Ian resolved.

Moments later, the door was pried open.

Ian shot at Zhowltagook's feet from under the bed on the other side. He tapped the button in the middle of the middle row. It activated what Ian called the "Push-back".

Zhowltagook was off his feet and he sprawled across the floor. Alexis had immediately gotten up and taken the chair from the desk. Drake complained, but the response was ignorance.

She took it and threw it down on Zhowltagook. He became unconscious, and that was their chance to leave.

They found an exit and into a park where there were heaves of leaves that had been raked into piles.

The piles were awkwardly shaped.

One exploded next to him, leaves raining onto him. That caught his attention as an unknown person grabbed his ankle and he was yanked onto the park's lawn.

He felt being heaved up and steady again on solid ground. A flock of pigeons had attacked the Dark Elf who had attacked him thanks to Alexis. Then, simultaneously, Dark Elves surrounded them from their hiding spots…the piles of leaves. It was a trap. Ian had an idea, which typically didn't come so fast.

There had to be a dozen piles of leaves at least. The Dark Elves brandished their bows. Ian raised his hand.

He turned in a circle and shot bolts of fire onto the grass. It was a distraction. Then, Ian alternated from pressing the "bolt of laser" and the "bolt of purplish-white something" buttons all around him.

After a few seconds, Ian activated the force field. An arrow bounced off and flew back like a boomerang at its shooter. It hit him and he fell. Ian retracted the "curved spikes" and ran, jumping over the flames and whamming a Dark Elf in the face with the flat side.

A military helicopter flew down to 15 feet from the park ground. It fired a machine-gun, getting rid of the remaining. The Dark Elves slumped onto the grass.

Faster than the eye can see, something appeared out of thin air and thrust a knife into Rosalyn. It disappeared right away.

Rosalyn fell to her knees and lay onto her side. She couldn't speak anything. Blood was oozing out of her wound and mouth. She wasn't going to make it.

Jocelyn fell to her side and hugged her, begging that she wouldn't die. But it was too much to take control of.

She was gone, and dead forever.

The second one she was. How many more would die?

Out of the blue, Ian knew Shadow Clan was part of this now. He had been in their territory. He understood their ways.

Ian spotted The Shocker a few blocks away.

"We've got to move and take cover. Staying in the open is not a good idea," Ian pointed out. Jocelyn was still mourning and sobbing. Aubrey hung his head because he knew her pretty well. "She was a lovely girl..."

Something flew overhead, and down onto them from the buildings. Ziknios. Ian led his team down the street as Ziknios flew in front of him. Some Dark Elves continued to fly off trees and tried to stop them.

Ian had run around for a few blocks before he realized not everybody was together. Only Alexis was with him.

He barely noticed The Shocker, flanked with Sloogpaps, coming towards them. "Alexis?" "Yeah?" "Let's go!"

She got the message. They were chased out of the city and into low rolling hills. Then, there were valleys.

Then, they started to cross streams. At last, Ian found a log cabin that didn't seem inhabited, which was good.

"The Forbidden Landscape is a place where there have once been a nuclear release of an unknown gaseous substance. That is why it is a prohibited place," Alexis suddenly said. "What? How do you know this?" Ian retorted. "Because...I pay attention to what is going on in the world, unlike you," she smiled for the first time after so long.

Her smile was intriguing.

Ian relaxed. He settled down in a rocking chair he found that creaked every time it moved. Alexis sat by the fireplace on a mat (carpet) on the floor that looked as if it hasn't been taken good care of or dusted for centuries.

At least they found some kind of shelter or hideout. "Fall is beautiful...take a look for yourself," Alexis pointed out the window. "Yeah, all those colors? Yup!" Ian replied.

Alexis walked out. "Wait! It is too dangerous!" Ian hurried out. She sat down on the hillside, facing the city. Ian took his spot next to her…

"I wonder where the others went," Ian said.

She shrugged like it didn't matter. "You are a good boy, Ian. What you did down there was incredible," Alexis told him. Ian was perplexed and very much puzzled.

Ian desperately wanted to start conversations with her but couldn't find a topic suitable for this situation. Nothing could dart out of his mouth as typically.

It felt good being with her. He glanced at Alexis several times because she was *so* pretty. He couldn't stop the habit.

So they sat there in silence, calming down and reflecting, deep in their own minds and thoughts.

Her presence was very soothing and pacifying. He wanted to stay put like this, but he knew sooner or later, they would just get back to feeling insecure as always.

That was just how it was.

Her brown hair lay in strands. The way she kept her mouth slightly open was attracting and hard to not look at. The way she narrowed her eyes too. Her face was so clean. Man, it was a bonus. Ian was worried that she would find out that he was glancing at her too much. So, he took sneak peeks at her instead.

He would tilt his head a bit and look at her with the corner of his eyes. He couldn't stop it while Alexis just stared forward at the horizon, and at the rising sun.

Ian finally stared at his watch and saw that it was 7:30 am. They had sat there for over an hour, which was unbelievable! "Time to go!" he announced. Alexis didn't budge. She seemed to be day-dreaming and not noticing the present. Her consciousness wasn't there.

"Hey, wake up! We should go now!" Ian snapped even though he didn't really want to. The sun warmed up Ian's body. She stood up, and together, they hiked down the path they came before. What was Kael like now? A piece of rubble? Has it been torn-down?

Had the battle ended? How long ago then? There were so many unanswered questions floating around Ian's head.

And then this one came: When can we go home? Ian feared this answer: Never! The answer to "Had the battle ended?" was NO! The battle had raged into the center of the city and downtown, now much less the coastal areas. There was an immense fog that swept over the trees. Everything turned white. Now what? How was he going to get through this?

Alexis' hand reached for his. He let her take it. Ian felt a pang of embarrassment. But how else was he going to walk through the dense fog? It was impossible otherwise.

They held hands to stick together while their opposite ones were stuck out in front of them. Ian felt his way through.

Hand-in-hand they moved. Ian didn't really know what to do now. He stepped several times into mushy ground, his foot sinking a bit and himself stumbling. "Must have been a mole," Alexis muttered.

How did she tell?

They were back, back to the scene. Ian let go of her hand, and at that point, he felt like losing part of his soul.

Ian always wanted to ask all the questions he thought was *legit* and not too "information-seeking" to Alexis. It would sound weird if not. But he always didn't find the courage too, even though they hang-around fine.

Then questions popped into his head. What the heck was the Anything Code? It felt like there were infinite possibilities. Was it even solvable? And why was the word "code" in it if it could or couldn't be true?

Determining what was true and real rather than false was too difficult. He didn't know where to start with the Anything Code. He was clueless in trying to solve it, and the process for it, and the steps it takes.

The streets were all silent. Ian and Alexis made their way until they stopped at a baseball stadium after hearing noises. They walked in through the main entrance and hid in the bleachers. Ian saw glimpses of people on the baseball field— his friends taken hostage.

Were his eyes playing a trick on him?

Ian exposed himself and spawned the force field at the same time. Humans working for The Haunter fired semi-automatic rifles at him, but the bullets just bounced off harmlessly.

If it wasn't for the force field, Ian bet he would be torn to shreds already.

Then, Josh, Drake, Aubrey, and even Jarret took over with his stun-gun. Ian dropped to the ground and lay there as bullets rain above him. He then charged towards midfield to second base. Jarret was having fun stunning people with his gun randomly, and at the same time screaming for his life to be spared. Before long, the surviving humans fled the stadium.

Then, Ian saw the drone fly by, and circling. It fired missiles at the tops of the stadium, causing the rubble to cave inward. The debris fell onto the field and completely occupying home base, third base, and first base.

Ian and his friends were trapped with nowhere to go and nowhere out anyway, which completely sucked.

Then, he realized the enemies were closing in on them. Where was the military anyway? This was their last stand.

Side-by-side in a circle, the members of the Crystal-Recovered Squad stood, completely surrounded.

They were mostly done for.

The enemy came, jumping around the wreckage towards them. Drake brandished his glaive. Ian shook his wrist. Josh cocked his guns. Jarret straightened his arm, holding the stun-gun and looking a tad afraid. Reeve was ready, bow in hand. Alexis stood in the middle, ready to call for animals. Lorry seemed like she was ready to show the world her taekwondo skills. Aubrey stood his ground. Jocelyn was prepared to fight to her death to avenge her sister.

It was a blissful moment.

Then, it started.

Drake swept and stabbed. Josh took them down quickly with the many rounds of ammunition available. Aubrey reloaded and fired his own. Jarret flung his stun gun at those who got too close, each shaking before they fell, unconscious. Reeve shot down those in the distance. Lorry ran at Ziknios and swept her foot across the air, knocking some out.

Ian zeroed-in on a challenger—The Shocker. He took his time spreading out across the wreckage and pacing towards them with those tentacles of his.

"Mr. Boris! I missed you a lot!" Ian mocked. The Shocker hovered in the air, suspended, taking into account the satire and parody. He pursed his lips and nodded. "Yeah, I missed my favorite student too…" Boris answered.

Ian attempted a punch right in the chest, but he was thrown back by one of The Shocker's dragon-like legs. He couldn't move, the pain was horrible. He was too dazed and his nerves all damaged. Meanwhile, The Shocker was taking his time walking to him. Step-by-step he went as Ian lay there, immobile.

Ian was angry at his lack of movement.

The tentacles reached toward Ian's face. They sparkled with electricity. This was a painful way to die.

Ian shut his eyes, waiting for his death to arrive. There was a shimmer of blue light and then The Shocker stumbling backwards and standing immobile himself.

Flix stood behind him. A sword's tip protruded from The Shocker's chest. "You killed my brother The Breaker, Ian! You shall die a painful one!" he said, before falling face-forward and next, he was dead.

Ian stood there in shock, like he was just stunned by one of The Shocker's electrical cords.

Flix held the sword, which looked like a special one cause of the blue glimmer edged around the whole blade.

"You…you…you SAVED ME!" Ian exclaimed, running to Flix and hugging his metal body. "How'd you know?" Ian asked. "Because I sensed it…"

"Wait for me," Flix started, and he disappeared. Next thing Ian knew was the F15 plunging from the sky all the way down and a dark blue shape on the top attacking it.

Flix.

The F15 crashed right in front of the stadium. Flix walked casually back in and patted Ian's back. "And that is how you do it…" he announced.

The rest of the minions had been easily taken cared-of. They had won the battle. It was over.

Ian walked to the beachside and Cliffside. The military was still there—treating the wounded and stripping the dead.

There was no sign of Zhowltagook or Lady Harsh in the open. Ian and his friends had won the battle, apparently.

And then his thoughts went to and lingered to the Dark Elf King (DEK). Where was he the whole time?

Somebody was walking around, passing out fruit cups. Ian took his and slurped the clumps of pineapples, honeydews, and cantaloupes into his mouth.

Ian picked his way through the rubble.

A man appeared next to him, saying, "Don't relax so fast, our job isn't done yet. It is not over. I am the Commander in Chief of the world, for your information." Ian shrugged.

Chapter Sixteen: The Onslaught

"We have decided to get rid of The Haunter by targeting and releasing an onslaught on Zark in a few hours," the World Commander in Chief explained.

"Already? We are not prepared!" Ian blurted, not very sure why. "We need to do more research and spying if there is…trust me! Take my word!"

"The decision is not about you," WCC replied coolly.

"No! I know what I'm doing…listen!" Ian begged and urged.

"We've told everybody about this, so it is too late, I'm sorry," WCC answered adamantly. "Just go with the flow…" "I disagree! I oppose! Doing that means sudden and immediate death! Please!" Ian cried.

He was ignored.

"Let's go, gather your friends and let's go, to stop more fighting and death," WCC ordered. "Find the blue plane."

And without further instruction, he left the war scene.

Ian stood there paralyzed.

Alexis strolled over. "So…what's next?"
"What do you mean?" Ian asked. "Where are we going now?"

"You heard…right?" Ian questioned. "You bet I did, that is crazy!" Alexis confirmed. "Right? Don't you think so?"

"Totally."

"Well, we have no choice, anyway," Alexis smiled unfavorably.

Josh walked over.

"Now what?" he asked.

✳ ✳ ✳

The Crystal-Recovered Squad along with the entire military were dropped off in the Forbidden Landscape a mile from what they say was the borderline of Zark.

They trudged as a long line southeast. A barbed-wire fence came into view with green mist lurking beyond it. It was a very long fence that seemingly had no end.

185

The head of the military put his hand in the air to signal for everyone to stop. "Now, on this day, we will fight off the evil that wants to gain control of us. Once we find a way through the fence, just run towards whatever structure there is. There will not be any rules, instructions, or directions. Got it?"

Men and women in caps and combat suits gave slight nods.

A truck rumbled towards them and stopped, a ramp leaving from the back. Panda and seahorse resembling creatures wobbled down. "What? Why are the Moygeri here?" Jarret shouted out. "They want to fight...the more troops, the better...common sense!" a fellow soldier nudged Jarret.

Soldiers were already hacking at the barbed-wire fence, creating apertures and tearing the loose pieces off.

"On a count of three, we all charge through that green mist! One, two, THREE!" the commander yelled.

People flooded in.

Ian made sure he stayed with his friends and his mom.

They were all running around crazily and aimlessly. Ian peeked around and saw soldiers falling to the ground with green mist all over their faces.

The green mist.

Ian remembered seeing bottles of them being thrown into his house. Were they deadly? And what did they do?

The green mist looked alive, flying about and randomly picking their next victim. There was no fighting it.

Then, there was Zark, a perfectly normal city that looked like Yart. Ian was confused. He expected something a whole lot worse in this evil place. Was The Haunter even evil at all? No, the perfect Zark was an illusion. It had to be.

Ian saw a palace, but it was on a floating piece of rock detached from the city and behind it, suspended in midair. "Ian, remember one of the four steps Flix told us? To burn down a sacred palace? I think that is the one…" Alexis pointed out.

"I don't know…there doesn't seem to be a bridge," Ian said breathlessly as he ran towards the city.

A piece of the green mist wisped past Ian's head and hit somebody next to him. He didn't know when it was will be his turn.

Ian had an instinct that he was supposed to get near to the sacred palace. "Guys!" he called to the Crystal-Recovered Squad. "We need to get to the far side of the city over to that place!"

They neared the city. Soldiers split up, but the majority followed Ian.

Then, battle raged.

Ian reached the cliff. The sacred palace stood 100 feet away. And between was open space and the sea at the bottom.

There were the remains of a bridge at the bottom. Ian didn't know what to do now. From afar, a window opened.

There was a man's body walking out onto a balcony facing the city. "Lanterncup! We meet at last! I am the heir to The Haunter. Why, you are so young! Know me as the Colonel."

"The Colonel?" Ian asked. "Yes. The Haunter has come to regain control of the world. After everything your ancestor Clive did, he wants revenge."

"And furthermore, remember the time when you found out that kid from the fallen plane was actually your cousin? He has the power to revive, and revived him because he thought he would bring you distraction. But your cousin was strong, indeed. He fought it and got the deal of a lifetime. He doesn't know this because we wiped out his memory..." the Colonel announced.

His voice projected from a speaker somewhere in the palace. How else could he have his voice magnified?

Ian looked at Jarret. He was quite stunned at the news. "Just accept it, it was part of the past," Ian muttered a tip.

"Your grandfather Clive did the worst thing possible. He summoned the dragons to attack The Haunter themselves as he watched. He would've never been able to do so without the help of them. It was unfair and partial. It wasn't part of the deal. Now The Haunter is back, and he will not make the same mistake," the Colonel reassured.

"How sure are you?" Ian challenged.

"You shall pay for this!" the Colonel cried.

Then, the Colonel disappeared in the green mist and reappeared.

This time, it was next to Ian.

Ian jumped back. Drake drew his glaive. Josh pointed his guns. Aubrey brandished his weapon.

"I do not mean any serious business here, so drop your filthy weapons now, or…" the Colonel ordered, and they did.

"Do you know what this green mist is? We have upgraded it by adding a highly toxic substance named Krakum. I'm sure you would love to try it out, right?"

Dark Elves appeared, each snatching one person. Ian was strangled up by a familiar face. It was the Dark Elf King.

"Colonel, what do you wish us to do?" DEK questioned.

"Wait, I want to kill them painfully. But first, let us give them a taste of Krakum, see if they like it or not!" the Colonel replied.

Ian had a hunch it would taste pretty bad.

He couldn't loosen himself from the grip of the DEK who had bulging biceps and triceps. Besides, he couldn't move at all.

"Now, Lanterncup is first!"

Ian lashed out at the gripping hands with his chest muscles but couldn't move at all. He was done for.

The Colonel stepped towards him with a bottle that looked like it was for spray paint. He got within 2 feet and sprayed it into Ian's face. "Now breathe it in! Enjoy it!" the Colonel advised, grinning.

It tasted as bad as it can possibly be. Ian gasped and sputtered, his spit flying onto the ground. The gas tore into his skin, creating a burning sensation. Ian kept coughing, and passed out.

$$* * *$$

Ian awoke, only remembering that he was at the same place he was the moment before. He saw that the mouths of several teenagers in front of him and a woman was moving, but he could only hear the voice of something in the air.

"Go, shove them off the cliff."

Ian went to take one of the teenagers, a male, and grabbed him.

Ian felt completely powerful. He loved the feeling of power as he beat up the teenager and dragged him to the edge.

The male was screaming something at him he couldn't make out. Ian just had one goal, and that was to shove all of the teenagers, the few adults, the kid, and the woman off the cliff one by one.

Ian got to the cliff and pulled the teenager around him. Ian was laughing but couldn't hear it. He was just laughing hard like this was going to be the funniest thing to ever happen in history.

And that was shoving someone off a cliff.

Ian stared at his victim, who was struggling to leave his grasp. Then his victim was still. The head of the male looked up and mouthed a few words that Ian could make out this time. "No, don't do this, I am your friend, please!" Ian read to himself.

Ian shook his head, merciless. He pushed the teenager forward, making his legs dangle over the cliff.

Then, he recognized that facial expression. It was the face that read disappointment. Ian knew he was doing something wrong.

Ian stared back at the still and disappointed face. Tears rolled down his cheeks. He couldn't do this. Ian attempted to fight it as he pulled the boy back up. Ian screamed as loud as he could so everyone could hear it.

And with that, he dropped to the ground. The memories came flooding back in. He had been possessed by The Haunter.

Sound came back too.

"It is over, Colonel!" Flix appeared in his realm, pointing a gun at his back. All the Dark Elves were taken down.

"You will regret your decision…" the Colonel turned his head as Flix shot one fatal shot. The Colonel dropped to his knees with bloodshot eyes. "The Haunter is good…" and he fell to his side, becoming still. The entire seaside cliff rumbled. Something was appearing from below the ocean. Ian watched in shock.

A metal creature with open spaces in its body rose from the waves. It had a helmet with horns at the sides of it, pointing back.

Behind the helmet was a green face and head with a ghostly glow. A massive breastplate covered the front.

It was a skinny robot that was all black and very thin.

In its right hand was a massive staff with a mace at the top and a green blade in the bottom half.

Surely, this was The Haunter.

"Ian!" Flix hurried over. "I heard something when I was shadow-travelling here about how you can complete the four steps I told you about. The Anything Code must be *literally* broken by being thrown through the little Circle of Fire at the peak of the palace. That is why the Anything Code is so hard to solve. It could be, well, *anything*. The answer was right before our eyes the whole time. The Code doesn't need to be cracked (solved), but literally *cracked*. It will trigger the burning down of the palace, which will complete the 3 of the four steps. I was thinking that you shoot the Anything Code at the Circle of Fire. You only have one shot, and…"

A massive mace pounded Flix into the ground. "Flix…, you have deceived me for these humans!" The Haunter cried.

"I created your race and you have betrayed me! I started Shadow Clan!"

The mace rose and Flix lay there, dazed and damaged. "You are doing the wrong thing, Lord Gantwan!"

"We should never kill…" Flix attempted to jump into the shadows, but then, the neon electricity he had in the body was suddenly zapped out of him.

Flix fell down, without energy.

"I am deeply saddened with you, you should pay for your crimes!" The Haunter or (Lord Gantwan) exclaimed.

Ian suddenly knew that The Haunter was the head of Shadow Clan. Why hadn't Flix tell him and his friends before? Was he embarrassed at the fact? It wasn't his fault.

"Ian, all I wanted to do was preserve mankind," Flix uttered weakly as a green blade came crashing down.

Ian screamed.

The blade went right into Flix's middle, completely tearing him to bits.

The Haunter or Lord whatever was doing this. He was taking Flix's life.

Flix's limp body thudded onto the cold hard ground below. He was only a pile of metal sheets and dust now.

Ian couldn't believe it.

The Flix he knew was gone, dead, and killed by his own maker. Flix had lied that Shadow Clan was there even before The Haunter. He somehow didn't want Ian and his friends to know.

But Ian was sure that Flix was the good guy. He was now reduced to a pile of foiled metal. He was GONE.

Ian tried to keep his fury at bay, tried to maintain it. But he really wanted to go up to The Haunter and punch him in the face, square. He desired to.

Flix would never be forgotten.

The Haunter was now spawning tornadoes from his staff as it whirled around. His feet were still in the water.

Ian shot at the Haunter with his Wrist Striker. The Haunter's left fist came sprawling down and punched a section of the earth, causing bits to fly into the air.

The Haunter swiped the green blade of his staff and Ian was forced to hop into the air or else he would lose his legs. Ian crouched and shot bolts of lasers, moving around constantly to get to different spots.

He was not giving up.

Ian turned around and saw the remaining part of the military hurrying to them. The Haunter spotted new threats and started to pound his spiked mace at the oncoming enemy.

Then, something came out of the water. It resembled a snail and a camel. Was it the Snamel? The Snamel rose from the sea and lunged at the back of The Haunter's body form.

The Haunter was not aware and went plunging backwards. The Snamel took over and fought The Haunter in the sea.

But before long, there was a slice of the green blade, and it left a deep gash mark in the side of the Snamel.

The Snamel howled and attempted to return to the sea, but was snatched by The Haunter. The Haunter drew the blade deep into its gut.

With one last dying cry, it fell and was submerged in the ocean.

Such a poor creature didn't deserve that. The Snamel was a mom and Ian remembered his encounter with her when she talked about how she was trying to protect her children. Well, now she was dead for doing something meaningful, Ian thought all this.

It was too sad to watch.

Ian turned around and saw that The Haunter's minions were closing up on them from the city. The Haunter itself was on one side while his minions were on the other.

They weren't going to make it out alive.

Ian knew he had to act.

At the top of his voice, he spoke. "Alexis, come! The rest of you, all of you I mean, cover me. This won't take long!"

Half of the soldiers went to fighting The Haunter, and the other half, his minions. Alexis went to Ian, looking puzzled.

"Listen, Flix told me something that can stop this all. I need your help to carry the Anything Code. My duffel bag is over there, go take it out. Then, I am going to fire the "push-back" and get it through the Circle of Fire over there. No questions now. Every second counts lives." Alexis retrieved the Anything Code and brought it to him. "Now crouch down in front of me and I am going to aim," Ian informed her.

A crowd of soldiers enclosed Ian and Alexis, protecting them. Ian knew that he was going to thank them one day with probably a free meal at a fancy restaurant, but for another time. Right now, he had some business to do.

One shot, Ian thought. Seriously? This was harder than his final exams at school! He aimed with his undivided attention. He didn't care about his surroundings anymore, just the fact that he needed to get this over with. If he failed, everyone would die. All the lives were in his hands now, including his own.

Ian focused and concentrated. He got into a comfortable position.

Alexis got ready her position too, looking apprehensive.

Ian steadied his wrist. He was never good at math but tried his best anyway. He measured the distance and length.

At the same time, he imagined the launching horizontal line as the 'x' axis and that it would move as a parabola, going up and then down.

Ian gave Alexis the heads-up. "Let's do this!" He shot the bolt of purplish-white bolt of something at the side of the Anything Code as it flew into the air.

It ascended to the climax and slowly fell, almost reaching the opening of the Circle of Fire. It went straight through.

Ian put his fists in the air and rejoiced, celebrating.

Meteorites fell from the sky onto the palace, completely engulfing it in flames. It was burning to the ground.

A leg broke off of The Haunter. The Haunter stumbled. "No!" The Haunter took some water in his hand and dripped it onto the palace, extinguishing some of the flames.

Then, Ian saw that his own duffel bag was shaking uncontrollably. He hurried to it, unzipped it, and threw the crystal out.

In a split-second, the crystal shattered, and something bright flew out of it, getting longer and bigger as it rose into the air.

The Crystal Dragon.

"Haunter! You were never supposed to be here. The Space Assigners said so! You were supposed to be assigned to that planet a million light years away but fought for earth because it was *prettier*. You abandoned your own planet to fight for one that you were not assigned to. I was here because I was assigned. You are here because you are jealous! The Space Assigners wanted me to look over the humans. You came to destroy the humans!" the Crystal Dragon spat. "This kid is amazing," he gestured to Ian.

Ian shrugged, a tad confused.

"Time for you to leave once and for all!" The Crystal Dragon shot out a beam of purple from his mouth at The Haunter's throat. "I will not kill you but banish you from the planet! Oh, be ready for those punishments and consequences you will get from our dearly Space Assigners!"

The Haunter was dragged out of the water and into the air. The purple beam lifted him up slowly.

"No! Please! I worked so hard…!"

Those were his last words before they were muffled by the clouds.

The purple beam disappeared and half a second later, the Crystal Dragon shot yet another beam that left its mouth and flew upward. "That should take care of it…"

The dragon turned its attention to Ian.

"Lanterncup, I never would have let you take that crystal, but thank you for bringing me all this way to unleash my fury on The Haunter. All I said was true. There are these spirits called the Space Assigners that includes him and me. I am just in the form of a dragon. But The Haunter rebelled and wanted Earth to himself. Now, may I return to my place in the Mountain of Day and Night?"

Ian couldn't believe this beast. He knew he was speaking the truth. "Yes," it slipped out of his mouth.

The Crystal Dragon rose into the air.

"Oh! And those who worked for The Haunter, go get lost before I devour all of you!" the dragon looked beadily at the Zartees, Sloogpaps, Moods X Happs, Dark Elves, etc. Oh, and Shadow Clan, stop all this commotion before I rip you all up with my claws.

"Oh! And Lanterncup, everything I just said was a total lie…"

The Crystal Dragon shot a few spikes out of its tail and brandished its claws. "Get ready to die!"

One of its claws smacked Ian and Alexis to the edge of the cliff. Alexis went over the edge, and out of fear, Ian grabbed her wrist before she would plunge.

The gravitational pull was too hard. Somebody was running towards them but fell onto the ground.

"I am sorry, Alexis, I can't take it anymore," Ian said with heaving breaths. He let go of the edge and they plunged together.

Chapter Seventeen: The Miracle

Ian hugged Alexis close to him, lifting her up to his chest to make sure she wouldn't feel the impact as hard as Ian would a half-second after letting go.

Ian tucked his knees under him.

He'd probably break a few bones.

The air was fresh and felt good on his skin. The sun warmed his body up. Ian didn't remember the impact.

He could feel losing his sense of touch and drifting down to the depths from the surface. His body was limp. His water-filled eyes watched the glow of the sun on the water, making it look blue rather than it being white.

Ian was resilient.

He tried his muscles and saw they worked fine. Ian dove back up to the surface, not feeling any pain somehow.

He could see the body of Alexis floating inches from the surface. Her eyes were closed. Ian grabbed her hand and yanked her up. They hit the surface.

Ian pulled her along to shore.

He found himself lying on the sand, feet still in the wet zone and opening his eyes. Alexis lay next to him with eyes closed. He put his hand where her heart was and felt. There was a beat, a distant one.

Ian could hear footsteps.

He craned his neck and saw a line of people with somebody in their arms. It was Josh. They settled him on the sand.

"He wanted last words," Drake said solemnly for some reason, resisting the urge to sob and cry.

Reeve was a mess herself. Her face was all red and absorbed with sadness, tears rolling everywhere.

Josh had a big wound in his back.

"Ian," the faint voice came. "They killed the Crystal Dragon with their guns…thank you for letting me be part of saving the world. Thank you so much…forgive me for everything I've done wrong in the past to you. Thank you," and with that, Josh rolled his head up to stare at the sky forever.

Ian lay there, speechless. He had lost both Flix and Josh.

But they both died knowing they had done something great. Ian thought of Joe and his dad Arnold, and all those that had died. They were the best.

Ian took a moment to thank every single one of them.

The world was like this thanks to you brave souls, Ian thought.

He knelt and stood finally. The world had survived The Haunter. Ian grinned at this. He sat down on the soft sand and looked into the distance. It was a beautiful view. What was he going to do now? Surely this event would go down in history, no doubt.

Ian couldn't understand why he didn't die from falling. It was a miracle, and he took some time to thank God for everything.

He was going to return to his old life now and go back to school. Everything would be back to normal.

Ian hugged Alexis close to him to conserve heat as he watched the horizon and the sun sinking below the skyline.

Until next time.

Epilogue

She walked down the aisle, all sweet and glamorous in her bridal gown towards a smiling man…Ian Lanterncup.

They were in a church and the minister was waiting with his Bible.

Ian was 22 now and waited near the stage in the first row of the chairs. He had just graduated from Yart Briar University that was built after the time known as "The Hauntian Reign" with a Bachelor's degree.

Grinning faces sat staring at the bride making her way towards him. Alexis. She was the one.

Drake was there with Ian, standing beside him with his newly cropped beard and mustache. Ian had combed his hair and was in a formal black suit.

Lorry was crying tears of joy and speaking to herself, "He is finally leaving me!" as she continued sobbing.

Ian thought of his dad and wondered how proud he would be if he was here. But all he could do now was stare into the brilliant face of Alexis who was reaching him.

Ian was a tad nervous.

He wanted to show the audience how much he loved her. The world had watched him rescue her before a decade ago because the whole scene was recorded.

Ian had become popular in spite of this.

Reeve was there sitting close to Drake and Jarret was a teenager now, beaming at Ian and stealing grins.

Alexis reached Ian and he took her hand. They stood with sides facing the audience and faces to each other.

The minister opened the Bible.

"We today come to celebrate the marriage of Ian Lanterncup and Alexis Vos," the pastor said. He then read a few verses including ones from the book of Genesis. The pastor read, "In Genesis 2:24, it says "For this reason a man will leave his father and mother and be united to his wife, and they will become one flesh." "So today, in the spiritual house of the Lord, let us congratulate this cherished marriage between the two that they live together helping each other out. There will be joyful times and also disagreements. Let them overcome those disagreements and resolve them together as one.”

“Now is the Ring Ceremony,” the minister announced, taking the rings from the cuddled hands of the ring bearer and putting one of each in their hands.

Ian gently took Alexis’ hand and slid the ring through her finger. Alexis blushed and took Ian’s hand, sliding hers into his finger. Ian smiled at her.

“You may kiss the bride!” the minister announced.

Everyone applauded.

Drake nudged Ian and gave him a heads-up for him to go for it.

Ian nodded, grinning, and put his hand behind Alexis’ head. He pulled her closer together and put his lips into hers gently.

Ian spun her around as he kissed her. This was true love.

After that, they walked back down the aisle to the front doors leading out into the foyer as the Canon in D by Pachelbel was being played on the grand piano. Ian wasn’t just feeling happy, but feeling everlasting joy in his heart. He was so happy he couldn't believe it. He barely saw his mom come up and hug him hard.

"Oh Ian, you are a good son…" and he was pulled away by several of his friends. "That was awesome!" Brad exclaimed. "Yeah, you were amazing!" Desmond cried. "Dude, you were so calm and *cool*!" Dale added.

"Catch up on you guys later!" Ian muttered as he was pulled away by Alexis' friends. "I am so happy that we are together!" she exclaimed. "Me too," Ian agreed.

They walked together to the limousine that would bring them to a banquet hall. He'd managed to get the Wrist Striker 280 off his wrist a few years ago. There was a scar on his wrist but wasn't too disappointed because it was a symbol according to Ian. The Wrist Striker 280 now lay in a case in his bedroom back at his new house. Drake, Reeve, and Jarret caught up with them. "Hey yo! Aubrey and Jocelyn sent you a text congratulating you two. I think they are a thing now…" Drake cheered them. "Well, tell him I said thank you. Too bad they couldn't come because of the hurricane. I hope I get to meet them soon…" Ian acknowledged. Ian felt good. He felt very good. Ian thought of his memories.

He thought about The Haunter and his reign. It was all too long ago. He needed to focus on the present and future, not the past.

The past was way back then.

The End

Acknowledgements

What a journey this series has been! I want to thank the Lord for giving me this incredible talent of writing stories and letting me enjoy it. I want to thank the people around me also. This series has been mostly from experiences, watching movies, imagination, and creativity. I cherished the moments of writing this book and the first three of the series. It was an exciting and thrilling ride to be on with many ups and downs. Now, it has finally ended. I hope you enjoyed my books. Hungry for more stories? Look forward to new ones in the future! Thanks to all, and farewell! I encourage you all to write stories of your own. Remember, every one of you shouldn't be afraid with sharing your thoughts even if you think they are extremely absurd and dumb. Every one of you is unique. Best regards from your favorite author, Marcus I. Tay.

www.ingramcontent.com/pod-product-compliance
Lightning Source LLC
Chambersburg PA
CBHW030449250626
47154CB00003BA/1191